TEXAS DAD

BY
ROZ DENNY FOX

D1334061

MILLS & BOON

Published in Great Britain 2014
by Mills & Boon, an imprint of Harlequin (UK) Limited,
Eton House, 18-24 Paradise Road, Richmond, Surrey, TW9 1SR

© 2014 Rosaline Fox

ISBN: 978 0 263 91278 4

23-0414

Harlequin (UK) Limited's policy is to use papers that are natural, renewable and recyclable products and made from wood grown in sustainable forests. The logging and manufacturing processes conform to the legal environmental regulations of the country of origin.

Printed and bound in Spain
by Blackprint CPI, Barcelona

"Have you even seen a horse since you left Texas?

"I thought once the cattle were calm you and I could ride out to the draw and back in one day. But if you haven't ridden in a while, you'd end up too saddle-sore to sit for a cross-country flight."

"Don't sell me short," JJ said, further irritated because the sight of his large hands around the can made her insides squirm. "Magazine photography isn't all glamour. I've trekked into some wild and woolly spots, and I always carry my own equipment."

"Touchy, I see," Mack drawled.

"You're darned tootin'." She tossed back some of the Texas lingo she hadn't fully lost. "I'm no hothouse flower, Mack. If I wasn't needed here today, I'd ride along and photograph your whole trail ride. And I wouldn't need special privileges."

"If it bothers you to stay behind with Zoey and Erma," he snapped, "I'll leave the guys to calm the herd and ride back here this afternoon."

"I'm not bothered." She drew back, giving him a puzzled look. "Are you bothered about leaving me here? Are you afraid I'll run off with the Bannerman silver?"

Roz Denny Fox's first book was published by Mills & Boon in 1990. She writes for various Mills & Boon® lines and for special projects. Her books are published worldwide and in a number of languages. She's also written articles, as well as online serials for Mills & Boon. Roz's warm home- and family-focused love stories have been nominated for various industry awards, including the Romance Writers of America's RITA, The Holt Medallion, The Golden Quill and others. Roz has been a member of Romance Writers of America since 1987, and is currently a member of Tucson's Saguaro Romance Writers, where she has received The Barbara Award for outstanding chapter service. She's also a member of Desert Rose RWA chapter in Phoenix, Midwest Fiction Writers of Minneapolis, San Angelo Texas Writers' Club, and Novelists, Inc. In 2013 Roz received her fifty-book pin from Mills & Boon.

To view her backlist visit her website at www.korynna.com/RozFox. Readers can e-mail her through Facebook or rdfox@cox.net.

This book is dedicated to my critique partners,
Cindy, Suzanne and Laura. They are avid readers
and talented writers. In addition to busy lives,
they make time to read and constructively point
out ways to strengthen my stories.
Thanks for being my writing cheerleaders.

Chapter One

"Seventh grade is so gonna suck." Zoey Bannerman flopped down on her best friend Brandy Evers's couch and accepted a bowl of potato chips. "Thanks. The Open House at the junior high was the worst! Did you hear that snarky Heather Reed say I dress like a cowboy? She said Jay Lowery and all his friends call me a loser."

"Who cares what Heather says? She's mean." Brandy looked fierce as she passed Zoey a can of soda before sinking cross-legged onto the floor.

Opening the can, Zoey let it stop fizzing before she drank. "Things would be way better if I had a mom. I even heard Erma tell my dad he needs a wife. I wish I could help him find someone nice."

"You say that a lot, Zoey. I dunno. My mother says you can't just go out and pick a mom. It's up to your dad. Maybe you should talk to him."

"He might think I don't love him. I do, but next year school will be different with coed dances and stuff. Dad and Erma think since we live on a ranch it's okay if I wear jeans and boots all the time."

"Your housekeeper makes the best cookies in the world, but she's my grandma's age. And Erma doesn't shop anywhere except at La Mesa's general store.

What about setting your dad up with Trudy Thorne? Everybody knows she likes him."

"She's so phony. Erma says Trudy's only interested in how much my dad and Turkey Creek Ranch are worth."

"Then how about your dad's veterinarian? You like Delaney Blair and her kid."

"I love Delaney and Nick, but I heard Benny Lopez telling one of Dad's new ranch hands that Delaney's hung up on some guy who lives in Argentina."

"Who?"

"I don't know. He sold Dad his prize bull."

"Weird. I wonder why they aren't married."

Zoey shrugged. "Don't ask me. If my dad wanted to date anyone from La Mesa, don't you think he'd have done it by now?" She munched a few chips. "Your parents are so happy together. My dad's been alone for a long time. He's gotta be lonely." She set her soda can on a coaster on the coffee table. "I wish a nice woman from someplace else would move to La Mesa. Someone who wants a family." Hesitating, Zoey added, "Someone who'd love my dad, but who I could talk to about clothes and…and…boys."

"But your dad would have to meet her and ask her out first."

"Like that'll happen," Zoey lamented, twisting one of her braids.

"My mom said she'd take me to a big department store before school starts again in September—a place where they teach people how to put on makeup. And she promised I can get my ears pierced. If your dad says it's okay, you can go with us."

"Thanks. But I keep horning in on you and your mom."

"It's okay 'cause you don't have a mom, Zoey. And

Erma doesn't even wear makeup, does she? Hey!" Brandy jumped up off the floor. "I have an idea. My mom gets a magazine called *Her Own Woman.* Last week her gourmet cooking club went on about a contest the magazine is running. With single men, one a month. My mom's friend Lacy Doran said readers go online and write up what they like about a certain man. Readers get picked by the magazine to meet the guys and deliver a check to his favorite charity. They go on a big night on the town, sort of like a date. I bet your dad qualifies. Wait, I'll show you."

She crossed the room and dug some glossy magazines out of a rack. Dropping down next to Zoey, Brandy flipped pages until she found the contest. The girls huddled together, reading.

"They need photos," Zoey said, frowning. "And an essay on why he deserves to be chosen. They've done January already. He's a skier." She opened the second magazine. "February is a mountain climber. Gosh, March and April aren't wearing shirts. I don't think my dad would go for this. And look…it says all nominees have to sign a release."

"Only if he's picked, Zoey. You can write an essay. It says they want a compelling story. Remember when Mrs. T. did that lesson in language arts about how certain words show emotion or sympathy or whatever? Just write that your dad's lonely and you want him to be happy. It can't hurt to mention that it'd be great if your dad makes the cut, if they'll send a woman who knows about ranching…and teenage girls."

Zoey mumbled, "I won't officially be a teen till November."

"Still, the sooner you put in a request, the more

chance your dad has to win." Brandy leaped up. "If they don't choose him, we'll figure out something else."

"Okay. Help me write. When I go home I'll start taking pictures."

"Let's go up to my room. I'll borrow my mom's laptop. If she comes in from her greenhouse, she'll probably say this is a bad idea. Moms are fussy like that, Zoey, I'm just saying."

MACK BANNERMAN STOMPED into the barn and began furiously pitching hay into a hay wagon.

"Worried about the drought?" asked Benny Lopez, who had been Turkey Creek's ranch foreman since Mack was a boy. "You'll feel better knowing I rode out to the spring that feeds Turkey Creek yesterday. There's water bubbling up. Your plan to drive the herd to Monument Draw May 1st should give them a chance to fatten up on sweet grass before we take them to market."

"Good. But it's not about the drought. It's Zoey. For three days she's been obsessed with taking pictures and it's driving me nuts. Every time I turn around she shoves a camera in my face. Today was the last straw. She barged into my bathroom when I was shaving and, bam, a flash blinded me. I cut my chin. We were both damned lucky I had a towel wrapped around my waist."

Benny threw back his head and laughed.

"I might laugh, too, if I hadn't had to give her a lecture on privacy. I hate scolding Zoey. Usually I support everything she does, but I'll admit I freaked out when she told me she wants to take photography classes in junior high. Maybe it's a passing fancy, but…" Mack sighed and leaned on the handle of his pitchfork.

"Ah, you're thinking about Jilly." Benny rasped a thumb over his stubbled chin as he eyed Mack, who winced. Benny's remark propelled him back to the time of his father's death from a massive stroke. He'd been madly in love with a girl from Lubbock, where they'd both attended college. They'd even been engaged. Jill Walker was a photography major who, instead of supporting him in his hour of need, returned his ring by mail and flew off to Paris to further her career. That much he'd learned from her mother, who said he should forget Jill. And he'd had to drop out of college to run the ranch.

"I rarely think of Jill," he muttered. "But since you brought her up, you can't blame me for not wanting Zoey to be a globetrotter?" Mack dug his pitchfork into the pile of hay again.

Benny grunted and went back to hosing out stalls.

Mack paused to rub his shoulder. Telling Benny he rarely thought of Jill Walker wasn't true. He'd completed his agriculture degree online, so he received the college alumni newsletter—which often touted Jill's accomplishments. And he kept two of her early photos hanging on his bedroom wall. One was of a sunset over South Padre Island that Jill had shot the weekend they first made love—after he'd asked her to marry him. The other, a picture of their group of friends, she'd taken on campus. She'd set up a tripod and snapped the photo via remote. They all wore sappy grins.

He should toss the pictures. For one thing, the members of the group had scattered, or worse. Tom

Corbin, a quiet, likable Yankee, had been killed in a
motorcycle crash a week after Mack's dad died. And
there was Faith. Her heart—damaged by childhood
rheumatic fever—gave out during childbirth. Memories of Faith always came wrapped in sorrow and
regret. Her life had never been happy. They'd dated
for a while in high school, in spite of fierce opposi-
tion from her controlling, too-pious father. Even after
they'd broken up because her parents were such jerks,
Faith's father had insisted she attend a religious college. In defiance, the next year she followed Mack to
Texas Tech. But by then he'd fallen in love with Jilly.
Yet, through a quirk of fate he and Faith had ended
up married. And Zoey—Faith's gift to him after so
many losses in his life—came as a blessing.

He let his vacant gaze cruise past Benny.

"Maybe you should take a day off, boss. Go into
town and have some fun."

"What? Oh, no, I was just thinking. Have you noticed how fast Zoey's growing up?" Mack's tone was
wistful. "I wish I could still pop her in that chest sling
I used—remember when the only thing that lulled
her to sleep was me riding around the lowing herd at
night?" He grinned. "She was so excited the first day
we let her ride Misty."

"I don't see her riding as much these days."

"No. Erma thinks it's a phase because of her age....
She mopes around. I don't know what to do, Benny.
And I see Erma slowing down when Zoey most needs
a woman's guidance."

"That's why Erma nags you to find a wife. If not
for your sake, Mackenzie, then for Zoey's."

Shoving a lock of dark hair off his forehead, Mack

stared out the open door into the nearby corral. "My heart's not in the hunt, Benny. My heart's not in the hunt."

PHOTOJOURNALIST J.J. WALKER rushed into the weekly planning meeting at the New York high-rise offices of *Her Own Woman* magazine. She juggled her morning coffee, a bulging camera case and a portfolio from her most recent fashion shoot in Cancun, where she'd gone after covering the Mardi Gras in New Orleans. It was already April. She'd been on location for a month, and if her office assistant hadn't reminded her about this meeting, she would have missed it. Settling into an empty chair, she took a big gulp of coffee, liberally laced with cream and sugar. When she glanced at the hundred-inch wall screen where editors were displaying upcoming layouts, she was bombarded by four up-close photos of a man she'd never expected to see again—the only man she'd ever pledged to marry.

Choking, she spewed coffee all over her skirt and new Dolce Vita wedge sandals, which even with her deep professional discount had cost a mint. She created a stir in the room as she noisily mopped up. When everything except her racing heart had calmed down, she asked, "Wh-what's with the, uh, cowboy?" She wanted to deny it, but she knew the pictures staring down at her were of a more mature, but still handsome, Mack Bannerman.

A beaming features editor loudly announced, "He's our Mr. August, J.J."

"Yeah, our Mr. *Hot* August," an art assistant joked as she fanned her face.

Though she didn't intend to give anything away,

J.J. blurted, "I thought all our featured men had to be single."

"I hoped you might know him." Donna Trent, the boss, turned in her seat to focus on the flustered J.J., even as the features editor went on to say, "According to the essay, Mackenzie Bannerman, Texas rancher, is very single."

Last year someone on staff had proposed featuring one man a month in the magazine. J.J. had been one of the few dissenters. She continued to shake her head. "I must have confused him with someone else."

Donna pounced. "Come on, J.J., he's from La Mesa. Your hometown is Lubbock. I know you've been home recently. Didn't you just help your mom move into an apartment in an assisted-living community? On the map, Lubbock and La Mesa aren't too far apart."

"Texas is big," J.J. mumbled. "Okay—I know *of* him. Everyone within hog-calling distance of La Mesa, which by the way is pronounced La-mee-sa, not La-may-sa, knows *of* Mack Bannerman. He owns Turkey Creek Cattle Ranch, the biggest Hereford breeding ranch in West Texas." Although what J.J. really wanted to say—that Mackenzie Bannerman was a two-timing rat—she couldn't without opening a vein and releasing years of pent-up heartache. She thought she'd vanquished those feelings, but apparently she hadn't.

"Perfect," her boss said. "Since you'll be interviewing and photographing Mr. Bannerman for his layout. He's a hit. Readers are already clamoring online for a chance to meet him, based solely on his entry photos."

J.J.'s heart dropped to her brightly polished toes,

now sticky with cream and sugar. "Assign someone else, Donna. I'm still jet-lagged from back-to-back assignments. I haven't had time to download the pre-summer fashions I took in Cancun yet."

"Joaquin is in Miami filming Mr. July, who's studying migrating sharks and dolphins. Our part-time photog is on maternity leave. I'd think you'd jump at the chance to check on your mom. I know you were worried that she'd have a hard time after losing your stepdad."

"True. But honestly, Donna, after taking a closer look, Bannerman's not all that photogenic. Let me scan our other prospects and find someone better."

The room erupted in hoots of laughter. "What's 'better?'" an assistant shouted. "He's gorgeous."

The creative director waved the essay, silencing the staff. "Everyone on the selection committee thinks it's so sweet, J.J. His daughter nominated him. She hopes we'll send the check for his charity with a nice lady who might make a suitable wife for her poor, widowed dad."

Donna broke in again. "This program has given us a huge jump in subscriptions. Almost triple compared to last year. If you write a story to capitalize on the sympathy angle, think of the publicity. Of course, we'll have to do our best to send a reader who ends up marrying him. That will make a fantastic follow-up down the line."

J.J. considered Donna a friend as well as a boss, but with Donna the magazine always came first, so she wasn't surprised by the suggestion. However, the notion that she'd participate in setting Mack up with some unknown woman was appalling. J.J. knew, of course, that he had at least one child. She was only too aware he'd had that child with Faith Adams, his former girlfriend. Although they'd betrayed her, J.J. had been sorry to hear about Faith's death.

The staff member with the essay said, "We'll screen the candidates carefully. It's obvious that his daughter wants her dad to fall in love and be happy again. And she's yearning for a mother, so we'll have to find someone nurturing. This poor kid lost her mother at birth."

That shocked J.J., who had specifically avoided asking about Mack on her trip home. And her mother, who hadn't wanted her to marry a rancher, would have never been the one to bring him up. However, the Mack Bannerman she'd known had been an intensely private person, and he'd be horrified to have a bunch of people mucking around in his life. *Unless he'd changed.*

She could still clearly recall the night thirteen years ago when she'd driven from Lubbock to Turkey Creek Ranch to tell Mack about a scholarship she'd been offered to study for her master's in photojournalism in France. She'd hoped Mack would ask to move up their wedding date; she'd have gladly foregone Paris to be his wife. But she'd walked in on a touching scene with her fiancé consoling his sobbing former girlfriend. Faith was blubbering about being pregnant, and saying that her very religious parents would, if not kill her, make her life miserable for what they'd deem a terrible sin.

Mack had tenderly brushed away Faith's tears, assuring her he'd speak to her father. Mack insisted Faith move to Turkey Creek straightaway. And he promised to keep her safe from her fire-and-brimstone preacher daddy.

J.J. had died a thousand deaths standing hidden from the entwined pair. She'd felt sick and humiliated to learn that Mack had gotten Faith pregnant. He and J.J. were engaged! The couple didn't see her leave Mack's house. She cried her heart out on the drive back to campus, but managed to harden it with help from her mother, who agreed to send back Mack's ring. Skipping graduation, she'd grabbed the Paris opportunity and hadn't looked back—until now.

She made one last effort to change Donna's mind. "What can we really know about the women who enter the contest? Who would want to meet a man that way? What's to say a winner isn't a gold digger, or…crazy?"

Donna rolled her eyes. "You know we run background checks on the men we feature *and* on the readers we select to deliver the five-thousand-dollar check. And everyone signs a release."

"Out of curiosity, what is Mack Bannerman's charity?"

The director with the application answered. "He underwrites a steak-fry festival each year. Proceeds go to a Texas contractor who retrofits homes for disabled veterans."

Impressed against her will, J.J. felt the last of her barricades crumble. Meeting Donna's steady gaze, J.J. murmured, "Fine. I'll wrap up this layout and go to Texas next week."

As the room emptied, Donna kept J.J. behind for a minute. "If the article and photographs go smoothly, take an extra week to visit your mom. I'm going on vacation for two weeks myself. When we're both back,

I'll help pick the reader we send to meet your Mr. Bannerman."

"Thanks. I guess I feel extra responsible because he lives in my home territory."

"Hmm. Is that all it is? I sensed it might be more."

"N-no," J.J. stuttered. "I pulled up my Texas roots a long, long time ago."

The woman gave a crisp nod, squeezed J.J.'s arm and walked out of the room, calling to someone in the hall. J.J. was left feeling rattled. *Damn it all, and damn Mack Bannerman for resurfacing from the rubble of her life and causing her to lie to a woman she admired—her boss, no less.*

Resolutely but by no means happily, J.J. flew across the country a week later. While in the air she decided how to handle this inconvenience professionally. Once she landed in Lubbock, she'd rent a vehicle, drive to La Mesa and meet Mack's daughter, as prearranged by staff. She'd ask the necessary questions to write an article, take photos of him on a horse herding cows or whatever he did during his workday. She'd spend one night in town, then go back to Lubbock and visit her mom. Afterward she'd zap straight back to New York—with her heart intact.

She had a plan, and she wasn't prepared for it to go awry. But late that afternoon when she checked into the motel in La Mesa, her plan did just that. The clerk at the front desk handed her a phone message from Mack's daughter, Zoey. The girl couldn't meet J.J. as arranged, the note said, because her best friend's mother couldn't bring the kids to town today. The message instructed J.J. to meet the girls at the public library at ten the next day rather than going out to the ranch.

Once in her room, J.J. stared out the window at the Western town that had grown little in the time she'd been gone. She admitted to being curious about the child Mack had with Faith. She hadn't known Faith well. It was Mack who had included the thin, pale woman in their college group. Sparing a moment to reread the message, J.J. felt a niggling suspicion that Mack might not be aware that he was going to be displayed in a high-circulation women's magazine. But she knew the staff had sent him a release to sign, so J.J. would meet the kids, then proceed. The staff of *Her Own Woman,* most of them mothers, had empathy for the motherless Zoey Bannerman. It hadn't occurred to them that anything might be amiss with the kid's nomination of her father. And maybe nothing was. This uneasiness in J.J.'s stomach could well be her own reservations over seeing Mackenzie again.

Had she known of this delay earlier, she'd have phoned her mom and taken her to dinner. Too weary now to drive back to Lubbock, she elected to go in search of food in town before calling it a night.

Fewer than twenty minutes later, a short walk down the main street from her motel, she sat at the counter of a hole-in-the-wall café, checking her messages while awaiting delivery of her order. It was frustrating as she kept losing her signal. Purely by chance, she heard Mack's name mentioned. A trio of rancher types in jeans and cowboy hats were discussing a year-long drought in the area that was of major concern, considering summer was just around the corner.

"If Bannerman has to sell his herd early and take

a loss, he might not be able to underwrite this year's steak-fry festival," the man closest to J.J. said.

An older man bobbed his shaggy gray head. "Be a shame if Mack had to cancel the event when more wounded veterans than ever need retro-fitted homes. Last year Mack raised funds to help three local veterans."

"Yep, I know. But our pastures are as dry as I've ever seen 'em in the spring," lamented a man J.J. couldn't see past the bulk of the others.

"Uh-huh, two bad grass fires already. Hey, Jody, how about a refill on the coffee," he called to the waitress, wagging his cup in the air. "And slices of that lemon pie all around? My treat," he told his companions.

J.J.'s soup and sandwich came, and the men quit talking to wolf down their pie, after which they dropped money on the counter and trooped out. J.J. found herself feeling sad to think Turkey Creek Ranch might be struggling. *And Mack.* He was the fourth generation of Bannermans to raise cattle. His great-grandfather was one of a few old-timers who'd built a Hereford herd with cows and bulls brought over from England. Mack had planned to crossbreed and produce a strain of hardier cattle more able to survive the extreme Texas weather. She'd once promised to support him in every way. Obviously he hadn't wanted her help.

She pushed aside half of her sandwich, wondering why she'd recalled that or anything else about Mack. It had taken her a long time to bury her pain.

Paying at the register, J.J. walked back to her motel, determined to put Mack out of her mind for the night.

THE NEXT MORNING, just past 10:00 a.m., she hurried into the library. It smelled like all the libraries she'd spent time in during her school years in Texas. The odor of pungent wax didn't quite hide the musty scent of old books.

The heels of her boots clacked on the weathered wood flooring. Rising late after sleeping better than she'd expected to, she'd hastily thrown on a citified version of cowgirl wear—skinny jeans, a sleeveless black linen blouse and understated gold accessories that were a staple when she traveled. Assuming she'd be driving to the ranch later, she'd pulled her hair in an easy twist that looked elaborate but really wasn't. It kept her hair contained and out of her face when she shot photographs in remote locations. Slung over one shoulder she carried her ever-present worn leather bag filled with cameras, light meters and other equipment she never found time to unpack between trips.

"I'm supposed to meet a couple of teen girls," she told the librarian. The woman pointed her to a round table partially hidden behind a counter on which sat two computers.

Crossing over to the waiting pair, J.J. smiled and said, "Sorry I'm a bit late. I'm J. J. Walker. I'm from *Her Own Woman* magazine." She was surprised that she couldn't readily identify which of them was Mack's daughter, given that she'd known both of the girl's parents. She'd forgotten Texas ranch kids tended to look younger and more scrubbed than teens she encountered on a New York subway.

For the girls' part, they seemed struck mute.

Not wanting to intimidate them, J.J. slid out a chair, dumped her bag on the floor and sat. "Well, I don't know who's who, but you know why I'm here. It must be exciting to have your essay and photographs chosen by our staff," she said brightly.

The girl with reddish brown braids sat up straighter. "I'm Zoey Bannerman. This is my friend, Brandy Evers. I took the pictures, and Brandy gave me suggestions for my essay." She kept her gaze downcast, which didn't allow J.J. to see if the girl's eyes were gray like Mack's.

Removing a folder and business card from her bag, J.J. said, "Our next step is for me to interview your father and take some professional photos. We want shots of him doing what he does every day on his ranch." Her gold bangles clinked as she spun her watch around to check the time. "If we head out now, I should be able to wind things down by four o'clock."

"Today?" The girls shared a look of consternation. Before J.J. could decipher it, the front door to the library flew open, creating a cool breeze. J.J. saw both girls stiffen as a man's deep voice called, "Zoey." Zoey jumped up and almost fell over the camera bag.

Leaning down, J.J. tucked the bag farther under the table, then let her eyes track over scuffed cowboy boots, up worn blue jeans, to a shiny belt buckle. Panic set in when she completed the journey and got stuck on the tanned, lean face of none other than Mackenzie Bannerman. Thankfully, he wasn't paying any attention to her, and that gave her time to take a deep breath and pull herself together.

"You should've let me know you girls were coming into town, Zoey. I expected you to be at Brandy's house. Erma fell down our back steps. She may have broken her hip. I had to bring her into the urgent-care clinic, and I wasted precious time tracking down Brandy's mom, who didn't hear her phone. Since I'm here, she asked if I'd drive you kids home. So grab your books and check them out. I have to swing back to the clinic to get the verdict on Erma."

The girls remained glued to their spots, Zoey standing and Brandy seated across from J.J.

"What's wrong with you two? Hop to it. Whether or not Erma broke her hip, she's going to be laid up for a while. I need to stop by the employment office and see if they can scare us up a temporary housekeeper." Only then did Mack seem to realize there was someone else at the girls' table.

J.J. knew the exact moment he noticed her—and recognized her—because his breath escaped his lungs in a hiss. He reeled back on his heels and swore out loud.

"Mack," she said, inclining her head ever so slightly to meet those incredible eyes. "It's been a long time." J.J. prided herself on the fact that her voice wasn't shaking like her insides were.

Fury wafted off the man and surrounded them in oppressive waves. J.J. could barely breathe for the tension that crackled between them. But of the two of them, she'd at least managed to be civil. Perhaps Mack—the cheater—didn't have it in him to do the same.

Chapter Two

Mack felt as if he'd gone back in time. He shut his eyes and opened them again slowly to see if he'd lost his mind. His heart was beating so fast that he wondered if he was about to suffer the same fate as his father—a stroke.

Nope, he wasn't living a nightmare. There sat Jill Walker, looking more gorgeous than she had at twenty-one. Pulling himself together, Mack snarled at her out of renewed anger—how dared she waltz back into his life when she'd treated him so abominably? "Jilly," he said icily. "What brings you to La Mesa? And why in hell are you with my daughter?"

Handing him a business card, Jill stared coolly at Mack. "I go by J.J. now...J. J. Walker. Believe me when I say I'm not here by choice. I'm on assignment. I assume you're familiar with *Her Own Woman* magazine, since Zoey nominated you and you were selected to be our featured man of August." She noticed then how the girls were frantically trying to signal her. She stopped talking, unsure what they were trying to convey.

"If that's not total bullshit, I don't know what is." Mack crushed her card in his hand.

The girls swooped around him at the same time the librarian hurried over to shush them. "You four need to take your noisy discussion outside," she ordered. "There are people here trying to concentrate."

Giving J.J. another angry glance, Mack collected the girls' books and bags, and hustled Zoey and Brandy out.

J.J. gathered her folder and camera bag, slower to follow. No matter how prepared she thought she'd be to see Mack, he was far more potent in person than in those photographs.

Mack and the girls stood at the base of the library steps when J.J. descended. He was waving his hands, and as she got closer she heard him demanding answers from Zoey. Huge tears rolled down the girl's face while her friend stood to one side biting her lower lip. J.J. might not want to be here, but she felt sorry for Mack's daughter.

"Girls." She broke in. "I suspect you haven't been up front with Zoey's father regarding my magazine's contest. The truth is we can't feature anyone who objects. In fact, Zoey, the magazine mailed you a release you were instructed to have your dad sign."

"I, uh, we… Brandy and me thought he could sign it later."

"I've got no intention of signing anything," Mack said, glaring down his nose at J.J. as he hooked his thumbs over his belt. "Release for what? What's going on? I didn't enter any contest."

"Nothing," Zoey wailed. "Everything's ruined. I didn't think you'd win, but if you did I planned to surprise you."

"That you have succeeded in doing," Mack said, drawing out a long sigh.

Brandy slid in next to Zoey. "Zoey did it for your steak-fry, Mr. B. Every winner gets a check from the magazine for his favorite charity."

Zoey scrubbed her wet cheeks. "The magazine people choose a reader to bring the check. And they send you and the reader to a nice restaurant…kind of like a date. Oh," she sobbed, "it's hopeless. Now you'll never go out with someone nice who can help me dress like a girl," she cried. "Next year Heather Reed and all the boys will keep laughing at me."

Mack stood in stunned silence a moment, unable to process the bulk of Zoey's ramblings. She was more upset than he'd ever seen her, and her sadness cooled his anger the way nothing else could. He used his thumbs to wipe away her lingering tears. Kneeling, he pulled her close.

J.J. noticed how his demeanor changed and his face softened when he gently tugged one of Zoey's braids.

"You look like a girl," he murmured. "Who says you don't? Help me understand, Bug. What check? What reader? Why do you think that girl laughs at you? And why does it matter if I date or not?"

"Don't call me Bug. Boys are bugs. Brandy's mom and dad call her honey."

Slanting J.J. an embarrassed little smile before he cradled Zoey's splotchy face in his big hands, Mack murmured, "I've called you Bug since you were born, because you were cute as a bug. If you don't like it, I'll stop. But the rest, especially the dating part, isn't a subject to be discussed in public."

Brandy interrupted again. "Mr. B., how come you know a magazine photographer from New York?"

He didn't answer, still peeved as he switched his focus to J.J. "I swear this is the first I've heard of any of this. I have no idea what's going on. I probably should have asked Zoey why she was stalking me with a camera a few weeks ago. But tell me how any reputable magazine can encourage children to invade a person's life without obtaining that person's permission?"

Beginning to steam at Mack's holier-than-thou attitude, J.J. flipped her folder open and yanked out a blank sheet of paper. "Like I said, the rules state that candidates must sign a release. The girls followed the rules. Our staff found Zoey's essay compelling, and the photos, well, intriguing. I was on a shoot out of the country when the decision was made to put you in the lineup. But no problem, Mackenzie, we can end this ASAP and I'll be on my way home. All I need is for you to jot a brief note declining to be included in our promo." She shoved the folder and pen toward him as he knelt in front of Zoey.

He reached up for the folder. Zoey looked stricken.

Gesturing with the pen, J.J. said, "By declining, you will forfeit the five-thousand-dollar donation to your charity. I imagine that's the biggest shame, especially if you're forced to cancel your steak-fry. I admit I was impressed by your charity."

"Forced to…? I'm baffled as to why you'd think there's some doubt about me underwriting our annual steak-fry." His expression even more confused, Mack rose to frown first at J.J., then Zoey. "Zoey, please stop crying. I've left Erma in the E.R. and we need to go see about her."

"Do you mean Erma Fairweather?" J.J. asked.

"Yes."

"I'd love to see her. Oh, but she probably won't remember me. I always liked Erma. I hope she's okay."

"You liked her, yet you had no trouble dropping out of her life and mine?"

J.J. flared at his unfair assessment, but rather than strike back in front of the girls, who were clearly hanging on everything passing between her and Mack, she bit back her comment.

Following another uncomfortable silence, punctuated by Zoey's sniffling, Mack threw up a hand. "Enough! Let's take a minute and get to the bottom of this. I hate seeing you so upset, Zoey." He knew he'd never handled her tears well. And Jill Walker seemed far too anxious to be rid of him. The way she'd stomped on his heart before blithely abandoning Texas still rankled. Having her here felt like unfinished business to Mack and he disliked leaving things undone. Maybe he'd reconsider this stupid contest for no reason other than to annoy the hell out of Jill—or at least put himself in a position to finally extract a bit of revenge.

"Don't everyone rush to explain," he said. "How about I take a look at the entry the girls sent in?" Mack held out his hand to J.J.

Thrown off-kilter by his turbulent gray eyes, she leafed through her folder. As she did, she chanced a glimpse at Zoey. The pleading expression in the girl's teary eyes left no doubt that Zoey didn't want her dad reading the story she had concocted. Could it be that

Mack wasn't aware of how much his unhappy daughter wanted a mother? J.J. recalled incidents from her own childhood, things her mother later claimed she'd done for the sake of giving J.J. a normal life. When the truth came out, J.J. had been resentful. Despite that, she wasn't here to offer the Bannermans advice or otherwise interfere in their lives. She wasn't a psychologist. But…Zoey looked so miserable, the very least J.J. could do was avoid causing added anxiety.

"I have the photos, but apparently not the essay," she fibbed, carefully extracting the four-by-six photos taped to a blank page. She passed it to Mack, and watched both kids sigh in relief.

Mack studied the top two prints dispassionately. He cringed when he got to the one at the bottom—the one Zoey had taken of him in the bathroom.

J.J. noticed a crimson blush rising up his neck and staining his tanned cheeks. He tugged on one ear, and she recognized it as an old habit of his, especially prevalent whenever he felt uncomfortable. She used to consider it an endearing trait in a guy who was tough in other ways. Her veneer of disinterest started to crack. Perhaps Mack wasn't so changed from the man she'd once known and loved, after all.

His color still high, Mack handed back the photos. "I can't pretend to have a clue why Zoey pulled this little stunt. I'm a rancher, not a male model, for God's sake. Zoey, you said you planned to take photography in junior high next year. If that's true, I can't imagine your teacher approving of a student doing this." He stabbed a finger at the pictures J.J. was busily tucking away.

Brandy was the one to answer. "The fact that Zoey's photographs were good enough for New York magazine people will impress teachers, Mr. B." She grinned while Zoey only looked more uncomfortable.

J.J. was beginning to find the whole thing amusing, since Mack didn't see himself as hot the way *Her Own Woman*'s staff did.

J.J. didn't like the contest, either, but for now she would keep the girls' secret, mostly because she liked seeing Mack stew over his decision. Clearly he loved Zoey and didn't want to disappoint her. How could J.J. not give the guy points for that?

Mack checked his watch. Again he frowned in obvious frustration. "Bug, uh, Zoey, I wish you kids had talked to me before you did any of this. But if you entered me hoping to earn money for my charity, I guess your hearts were in the right place."

Zoey hunched into her shirt collar. "I'm sorry. We didn't think you'd totally hate it if you won. I thought it was cool that the magazine picks a reader to bring your check. I thought you'd like a nice woman to go out to dinner with."

"But why not enter some young guy like Trevor?" Mack asked, referring to the younger of his ranch hands.

"I heard Mom's cooking club talking about the contest," Brandy admitted. "You sponsor the charity, Mr. B., so you're the one who needs to be in the magazine. Last year our class collected stuff like toothpaste and deodorant to send to soldiers. The teachers talked about how you give money to build homes for hurt veterans, so Zoey and me wanted to help get you more money."

J.J. saw Brandy dig her elbow in Zoey's side, which

prompted that girl to nod vigorously. "Yeah," she agreed, her big hazel eyes still glossy with tears.

J.J. rolled her own eyes as she listened, sure Mack was being manipulated. The girls were cute as could be, but what a pair. She saw Mack begin to cave and wondered if the kids knew to quit digging themselves a deeper hole when they might be winning.

"Hmm. So, it's only a one-time story in your magazine, right?" Mack's eyes bored into J.J.

She could lay out his daughter's real reason for sending the essay and scare him off, or she could give the girls a break. She'd probably come to regret this later, but she elected to play along for Zoey's sake. "One time, yes. Each monthly winner gets a four-page spread in the center of the magazine. Yours is slated for our August issue, with a follow-up on the check presentation the next month. I can give you our web address if you'd like to see the other men we've worked with. Basically I interview you and write an article about your life, your work and your charity. We'll include photos of you on a horse and with your cattle, like the pictures Zoey provided, but professional." She shrugged, figuring he'd bolt for sure if she said readers specifically liked beefcake.

"Well, about the photos Zoey took…" He scowled. "Just so it's clear…I don't usually work around the ranch without my shirt on."

"So, are you gonna do it, Daddy?" Zoey asked, hope creeping into her voice.

Mack was still teetering. He didn't want Jill Walker here. He certainly didn't want her poking in his life. He didn't want her following him around the ranch. But, dammit, neither did he want her to go before he had a chance to ask why she'd dumped him so unceremoniously when he thought they'd settled on a life together. Not that it mattered after all these years. Common sense said Jill wouldn't be straight with him, anyway. But his common sense fled as he faced her. She still had the power to ignite ripples of desire no other woman had sparked in more years than he could count.

"All right," he said with a sigh. "I'll agree because the girls already did what they did, and because your magazine shelled out some bucks to send you here. So I'll go along with it, Jilly—uh, J.J."

Zoey and Brandy discreetly bumped elbows, a move so practiced that J.J. guessed it held special meaning for the friends.

J.J. separated another page from her folder. "First things first. Sign and date this release giving me permission to proceed. I'll scoot on out to the ranch for a few tests with my light meter while you check on Erma. This shouldn't take more than a few hours to wind up."

Nodding, Mack ran a thumb over his lips before he took the pen she held out to him. He scribbled his name where J.J. indicated. As he jotted today's date he was starkly reminded of how many years had passed since this beautiful woman had hurt him so badly. He needed to keep his distance and be vigilant about not letting her hurt him again. Him *or* Zoey. Mack recognized hero worship in both girls' eyes, and he was already regretting his decision.

"Shouldn't Ms. J.J. ride with us so she can find our place?" Zoey asked, sunny again.

"My rental car has a GPS system, Zoey. I left it at the motel, but I'll be fine on my own," J.J. said.

Mack's cell rang and he excused himself, turning his back as he took the call. They all saw him massage his neck and heard his tense voice, so their chatter ceased. J.J. was afraid it was bad news about Erma. Instead, he exclaimed, "Trudy, this is a surprise.... Uh, Erma's still in the E.R. How did you hear about her accident so quickly?...It's kind of you to, uh, want to rush to the ranch to help out.... Really, there's no need. Thanks, though....Hey, sorry to cut you off, but I'm heading to the clinic for a verdict on Erma." He closed his phone, straightened and turned in time to see Zoey and Brandy making ugly faces.

"Girls! That's rude. Erma might have a few things to say about Ms. Thorne, but she has a good heart and was just being neighborly."

J.J. alone caught the mock gags the girls exchanged, because Mack had dug out his keys, dropped them and had leaned down to retrieve them. On rising, he motioned the girls toward a big, black, extended cab pickup. J.J. had already guessed it belonged to him based on the chrome cowcatcher bolted to the front bumper.

Zoey stopped, looked back and waved shyly. "See you, Ms. J.J. I like your boots a lot," she added. "I hope you don't mess them up tramping around our ranch. We have a lot of dirt."

J.J. smiled. "Please, girls, call me J.J. without the 'Ms.'" She cast a glance at Mack and interrupted him in the act of checking her out from head to toe. She felt her cheeks grow hot. Her boots were fashionable, with high heels, but they were black leather and should wipe free of dust easily. "I can wait and photograph you with your cattle tomorrow. I brought sneakers and a sturdier pair of boots for navigating around cow patties," she said, flashing him an exaggerated smile.

CAREFUL TO CONCEAL his real thoughts, Mack hoped his face didn't show the admiration he felt for how fantastic she looked. So good, in fact, his heart skipped several beats. Jill had always had a knack for enhancing her natural beauty. Once, she'd been his life. His love. For a year or so she'd been a favorite around the ranch. His dad, Erma and Benny all loved her. Then, poof, she'd up and run off, leaving him to grieve the loss of his father and her at the same time. Standing near her now, watching how the sunlight made a halo around her honey-gold hair, it was easy to forget how cruelly she'd walked away from everything they'd pledged each other. His question remained—why? Again the answer punched him in his gut—to further her career. Hadn't her mother admitted as much to him? Mack hated that even now her smile turned him inside out.

Zoey called for him to unlock the pickup. That brought Mack crashing back to the present. Stepping aside, he said curtly, "There's something we need to get straight, Jill. Take your photos and ask me any questions you have. Don't bother Erma if she comes home, and don't involve Benny Lopez. And stay away from Zoey."

Spinning on worn boot heels, Mack strode to his vehicle and jumped in. In his haste to leave the woman who shaded her stunning blue eyes as she watched his departure, Mack flooded the engine.

Zoey and Brandy had climbed into the backseat of the king cab but had yet to buckle in when Mack reversed sharply out of his parking space. His jerky move knocked the girls together.

"Slow down, Dad! You didn't give us time to fasten our seat belts."

"Sorry." Mack braked and studied the girls in his rearview mirror. "I told Erma I'd collect you from the library and come straight back to the E.R. I certainly didn't expect to be confronted by..." Cutting off his admission, he again took off too fast.

Brandy leaned forward. "So, Mr. B., you didn't get around to telling us how you know J.J."

"Yeah, Dad, it's weird, but cool, too."

"It's a small world, girls. Jill, that is, Ms. Walker and I went to the same college a long time ago. Most kids who graduated from La Mesa High went to Lubbock. And Jill grew up in Lubbock." He wouldn't call their recent encounter cool. He'd call it a punch-to-the-gut shock.

"Oh," Brandy murmured, sliding back in her seat. "My folks met in college, too, and fell in love. They lived in Utah."

"Here's the clinic." Mack jockeyed his pickup into an open slot between two subcompacts. "I'll go see what's up with Erma. You two stay put. And don't open the doors or you'll set off the alarm." Mack removed the keys, slid out and hit the automatic lock on his key chain. He hauled in a gulp of fresh air, glad to take a break from the kids' interest in him and Jill. Of all the photographers in the world, it was more than weird, as Zoey had said, that Jilly was the one sent from New York to handle a stupid contest his daughter shouldn't have entered in the first place.

As he stepped into the clinic, Mack curled a hand around the back of his neck to soothe the throbbing headache that had begun at the library. Stopping at the reception desk, he said, "I brought Erma Fairweather here. Is she ready?"

"Ms. Fairweather is still in X-ray. She should be finished shortly. We've been swamped today—we're blaming last night's full moon," the woman said with a twinkle in her eyes. "E.R. visits double when the moon is full."

"I've heard that about the full moon," Mack said. "More cows drop calves then, too. I'll be over there if you need me for anything," he said, pointing to an empty chair by the window. "I left my daughter and her friend in my pickup, so I want to keep an eye on them."

"Help yourself to coffee," she said, stabbing a finger toward an alcove where Mack saw an industrial-size pot. Coffee sounded good. He went over and poured a cup. He'd always drunk his coffee black. Oddly, he remembered Jilly laced hers with so much sugar and cream it couldn't even legitimately be called coffee. *A stupid thing to dredge up.* But he wondered if that habit of hers or other quirks he recalled had changed.

WAITING IN THE truck, the girls were quiet until Mack disappeared into the hospital. "I hope Erma's all right," Zoey said. "If her hip is broken, d'you think my dad will have to hire someone else?"

"Not Trudy Thorne." Brandy grinned.

"Unless he's desperate. Erma does all our cooking, and for Benny and the cowboys. She cleans everything. I don't want to do my own laundry!"

"Broken hips are serious, Zoey. If Erma can't drive, you may have to come school shopping with me. Or I guess your dad can take you."

"Oh, my gosh. My dad has no clue what girls wear."

"Speaking of that...isn't J.J. about the coolest lady you've ever seen? Well, except maybe for Lacy Doran. Lacy flies to Dallas for Neiman Marcus sales. I'd love to do that, but my folks say it's stupid to spend money on planes to go clothes shopping. When I'm grown up I'm gonna be rich so I can buy *all* my clothes at Neiman."

"Didn't you love J.J.'s earrings, Brandy? She probably shops in fancy stores in New York."

"She's an old friend of your dad's, Zoey. You should ask her to take you shopping before she leaves."

"I don't know if they're friends." Zoey worried her lip. "My dad didn't sound friendly when he saw her sitting with us."

"He acted weird. She kinda did, too. Like my mom and dad after they argue, before they make up." Brandy nudged Zoey.

"I guess I didn't notice 'cause he was mad at me, too. My dad finished college before I was born. That's a long time to stay angry at somebody, Brandy."

"Do you think the magazine sent someone who used to know your dad on purpose? You *did* ask them to send a possible mom."

"Yeah...the reader who delivers his check and goes on a date with him, not the person who writes the article for the magazine."

"I'm just saying, J.J. had cool jewelry, but no wedding ring," Brandy pointed out.

Zoey's mouth turned down. "Except J.J.'s only gonna be here a day or so."

"But if Erma's hip is broken, maybe J.J. would stay longer. J.J. said she likes Erma. Plus, she didn't give us away to your dad."

"Lucky for me."

"Zoey!" Brandy shook her head. "Think, okay? Hang around her until she leaves, and ask her advice about taking pictures. Maybe she'll take you to get your ears pierced. She wouldn't have to stay long to do that."

Zoey's frown turned into a smile. "What would be perfect is if I could convince her to stay long enough for my dad to start liking her."

"You mean, like…fall in love with her?"

Zoey nodded. "But how?"

"Well…I'll do a Google search on *love* and see if any ideas come up."

"Would you? My dad has our internet blocked. I can't exactly tell him why I want to look up *love*." She wrinkled her nose.

"I'll call and tell you what I find out, okay?"

The girls high-fived and bumped elbows in their special signing-off code. Giggling, they changed the subject, talking instead about the party Brandy hoped her parents would let her have for her upcoming thirteenth birthday.

As Mack stood by the window, he saw the girls chattering a mile a minute, and he was glad the Everses were such nice people. He counted himself lucky that Brandy and Zoey had gotten along like sisters from the day they met in third grade. Dan Evers sold tractors in town. His wife, Amanda, loved gardening. They'd moved to La Mesa and bought the old Thompson ranch so she could set up greenhouses. Several days a week she sold flowers and seasonal vegetables to local residents. Although Erma used to tend a large garden at Turkey Creek Ranch when Mack was a kid, she bought fresh produce from Amanda now. He knew she was slowing down.

He heard louder voices and turned in time to see a technician pushing Erma, in a wheelchair, into the waiting room. Mack tossed his empty coffee cup in a nearby wastebasket and rushed up to her. "How do you feel? What's the verdict?"

A harried-looking doctor showed up before Erma could answer. He handed her a prescription. "The pills are for pain," he said. Turning to Mack, he added, "She needs the pills for when the shot I administered wears off. I explained to Erma that her hip is badly swollen and bruised. I don't see a fracture, but I'm sending the films to a radiologist in Lubbock. I should have an answer in two or three days. This is no simple injury, and there could be a chipped bone. Of necessity, due mostly to Erma's age, I don't want her bearing weight on that leg for four to six weeks. This is a loaner wheelchair. You'll need to rent or purchase one and bring ours back as soon as possible."

"Mackenzie, I am so sorry," Erma said even as she adjusted a blue ice pack she held to her right hip and thigh. "I told Benny last week about that loose step. In my rush to gather eggs this morning, I plumb forgot about it and caught my heel. It was my own dumb fault."

Mack patted her shoulder. Taking in everything the doctor and Erma said, he was trying to figure out how they'd care for Erma and handle her many chores while she was laid up. His phone rang as the doctor impressed on Erma the need not to skimp on the pain medicine. "Take two of these as soon as you get home, and two more before you go to bed. Then the same dose twice a day until we get answers from radiology."

Excusing himself, Mack went into the entry to take the call. Benny's booming voice caused him to hold the phone away from his ear.

"Boss, where are you? Someone we were just talking about a couple of months ago showed up. She says you know she's here. It's Jilly Walker." The old ranch foreman whistled through his teeth—a wolf whistle that grated on Mack's already frayed nerves.

"Don't let her get too cozy, Benny. Jill is only a temporary pain in my butt. I'm with Erma. The doc's not sure if her hip is just bruised or fractured, too. But she's gonna be laid up for at least a month. We have to swing by the pharmacy for her prescription, and to see if they sell wheelchairs. I'll stop and see Leitha Davidson at the employment office. We need a housekeeper to fill Erma's shoes for a while. I hope they can supply someone. By the way, can you fix up some type of ramp into the house? Erma says she tripped on a loose board on the back steps."

"Dang, she told me about that last week. It's on my to-do list. But it came after hauling water to a thirsty herd, and bringing in cows with new calves."

"I'm not blaming you, Benny. This is our busiest

season. The last thing any of us need is to have Erma down, to say nothing of Jill messing up my life again. She promises it's for a day or two. Why she's here is a long story. I'll fill you in later."

"I might have a solution to one problem, boss. My cousin Sonja may be able to fill in for Erma. Sonja's youngest daughter just got married and moved away, so she's kind of blue. Hold off talking to Leitha until I call my cousin. She'd fit in here and I can vouch for her cooking."

"That's music to my ears, Benny. We'll be home within the hour. Let Jill, uh, take her trial pictures, and send her on her way." He ended the call and went back to fetch Erma.

Because Mack didn't really want to explain Jill's presence to Erma in front of the girls, he hurriedly mentioned the untimely visit as he wheeled the housekeeper out.

"Praise the Lord," Erma said.

"From my perspective it's more like a curse," Mack muttered as Erma's excited response made his heart flutter.

"What brought her back here?"

"Zoey and Brandy got it into their heads to enter me in a lame magazine contest. They won. Worse luck, Jill is who the magazine sent to do a story and take pictures of me around the ranch."

"Mmm, seems like serendipity." Erma shot Mack a broad smile over one shoulder.

"You're far too cheerful for a woman in your condition. I'll chalk it up to the pain shot the doc says he gave you. But there's one thing we all need to get straight. I am not the least bit happy to have Jill Walker land back in my life, even for a couple of days."

"Oh, I hear you, Mackenzie." Erma closed her eyes and tucked her chin against her chest.

Chapter Three

As soon as Mack unlocked his pickup with the remote, Zoey hopped out and ran to hug Erma. That pleased Mack. Zoey really was a good kid, although he should probably still dole out some disciplinary action for sending embarrassing photos of him to a women's magazine. He could take away a few of her privileges, he supposed, but he hated doing that to a lonely, only child. He knew what growing up alone was like.

"Zoey, will you please open the front passenger door? Stuff this bed pillow Erma brought under her right hip. Be gentle, she's in some pain."

"Is your hip broken?" Zoey asked Erma after her dad lifted the housekeeper into the truck. He folded the wheelchair and slid it under the canopy covering the pickup bed.

"The doctor won't know until a specialist in Lubbock reads my X-rays, Zoey. I sure hate causing your dad so much bother. He has better things to do than waste half a day taking caring of me. I made a dumb mistake, tripping over a board I'd already said was loose."

Mack boosted Zoey into the backseat, then rounded

the pickup to the driver's side. Then he said, "Come on, Erma. You're family. Dad gave thanks every day that you happened to be looking for work when Mom's cancer got bad."

"Such a long time ago. Twenty-five years," Erma murmured as she leaned back against the headrest. "You were younger than Zoey when your mom died, Mackenzie. The years sure roll on by quickly, don't they?"

"I was eight," Mack said softly as he pulled out of the parking lot.

Brandy rustled around in the backseat. "Gosh, Mr. B., you didn't grow up with a mom, either?"

Mack frowned in the rearview mirror. He was surprised at the old sense of loss that arose, given how many years had passed. "Zoey and I are lucky Erma landed at the ranch equipped to mother us," he told Brandy.

Erma stirred. "It was me who got lucky, y'all. You may remember, Mackenzie, but I was engaged to be married. My fiancé, Johnny, went MIA in Vietnam. It was right near the end of that awful war. I didn't have any real skills. Johnny's family and mine were both dirt poor. I attempted a series of odd jobs but couldn't live on what I got paid. Back then there weren't many good jobs available to rural farm kids. But I couldn't bear to leave La Mesa in case the army found Johnny. Since I wasn't his wife, they wouldn't have tracked me down. Seems like yesterday, but it's been forty years." She passed a trembling, wrinkled hand over her eyes. "Shoot, it's gotta be that danged shot making me lonesome. You kids don't need to hear an old lady ramble on."

Mack squeezed Erma's arm. "I've heard they're still finding dog tags over there."

They drove in silence for a little while. "What's MIA?" Zoey finally asked as Mack angled into a parking spot outside a chain pharmacy a ways out of town on Lubbock Highway.

"The letters stand for *missing in action,* Zoey," Mack said, preparing to climb out. "I'm going in to fill Erma's prescription and see if they have any wheelchairs— I'm hoping this pharmacy carries medical equipment."

"What about the wheelchair you put in back?" Zoey jerked a thumb behind her.

"It's on loan from the E.R. We can't keep it for the four to six weeks the doctor said Erma needs to stay off that leg."

"That long?" Zoey gasped. "Who'll take care of us?"

Mack reached back to tap her nose. "Aren't you ready to be our chief cook and bottle washer?"

Her eyes went wide.

"I'm teasing," he said. "I talked to Benny earlier. He has a cousin who may be able to help us out. Everyone keep your fingers crossed."

"I will," Erma said as Mack's door slammed. Silence filled the cab for a time, and it was plain to see from the way Erma's head fell forward that she was nodding off. Then Brandy whispered to Zoey, "How old do you suppose Benny's cousin is?"

Zoey shrugged. She kept her voice down, and said, "Benny's seventy-two. I know because Erma baked him a cake for his birthday last month. There wasn't room on the cake for so many candles, so Dad bought two in the shape of a seven and a two. Why?"

"Duh, our plan to find your dad someone to date."

"Yeah, but maybe I should forget trying to find a new mom. I forgot how young my dad was when his mom died, and he turned out okay. Erma took care of him. Maybe I'm being selfish. Am I, Brandy?"

"I don't know, since I've got a mom, a dad and all my grandparents. And from what you say about your grandparents, you don't talk to them, either."

"They're so preachy! If I had to live with them like they wanted, I'd never mention getting my ears pierced or learning to wear makeup. They think TV and cell phones are sinful. I'm lucky Daddy's lawyer fixed it so I only have to see them once or twice a year. And my dad goes with me." She shuddered.

The back gate of the pickup squeaked open. Peering out the rear window, the girls saw Mack slide a big box in beside the wheelchair. Then he slammed the tailgate shut and got into the cab with sufficient noise to jolt Erma awake.

"Are we home?" she asked groggily.

"No, sorry. I didn't realize you were sleeping, Erma. Here's your pain medication." She didn't reach out for the paper bag, so he asked, "Are you okay?"

"I think I need to lie down. I can't seem to keep my eyes open."

"We'll be home soon. Well, in fifteen minutes or so, after we drop Brandy off."

"Can she come home with us? I thought J.J. might take our pictures. For fun."

Mack ground the key in the ignition. "Jill will be long gone by the time we get home, Zoey. Plus I told Mrs. Evers hours ago that I'd collect you girls from the library." He passed his cell phone back. "Call your mom and apologize for how late we are, Brandy. Explain that the E.R. was superbusy."

Brandy took the phone. "I'm probably going to get my own cell for my birthday," she said, sweeping her long hair back behind one ear as she waited for the number she'd punched in to connect. "Wait, I have to try again. I wish we had better cell service."

They were on the road by the time she got through and relayed Mack's message, then passed back his phone. "Mom said thanks. She was picking tomatoes and lost track of time, anyway."

"Dad, can I get a phone for my thirteenth birthday? Some kids already have them."

"At twelve?"

"Yes, and if I had one you wouldn't have needed to bother Brandy's mom to find out we were at the library. You could have called me."

"That, young lady, is something you should have settled with me before you left the house. Responsibility doesn't start with owning a phone."

"Oh, brother," Zoey drawled, flopping against her seat back.

Mack pulled slowly down the Everses' lane. He beeped his horn at Amanda Evers, who was in her produce stand talking with a customer. "Erma, those tomatoes look great. Want me to send Zoey to buy some?"

Erma, who was dozing again, gave a start. She grabbed her hip and grimaced. "Darn, I'm afraid that pain shot is wearing off. Sorry, Mack, what about tomatoes? I, uh, thawed hamburger to make meat loaf. I sure hope I can stand long enough to fix supper."

Mack chewed his lip. "The doctor said to take two

of those pills when you get home, and he wants you off your feet. The kitchen counter is too high for you to work from a wheelchair, even if you were in any shape to make supper tonight. Zoey and I can figure it out after I haul water to the herd." Turning in his seat, he said, "Zoey, run and see if Brandy's mom has some lettuce and sweet onion to go with those tomatoes so we can have a good salad. I hope Benny's cousin can come ASAP." Digging in his pocket, Mack handed Zoey a twenty-dollar bill.

She crawled out and ran to the stand with Brandy.

Amanda Evers listened to the girls natter on about Erma's accident as she bagged produce, took Zoey's money and gave her change. "Honey, tell your dad to call me if he needs meals until he hires help. I'll round up neighbors to bring casseroles you can pop in the oven. Or better yet, tell your dad Trudy Thorne can come and stay at your place. She stopped by a while ago and mentioned Erma's fall. She wanted Mack to know she'd be happy to pinch-hit until Erma's up and around."

The girls traded a dark expression that Brandy's mom intercepted. "Girls, be nice. I realize some people think Trudy is pushy, but she probably has a lot to offer you and your dad, Zoey. Brandy tells me you're feeling the loss of your mother a lot lately. And the teen years can be rough. Trudy spent her teens here in La Mesa."

"Yes'm," Zoey said, although she pursed her lips. "I'd better go. Erma needs to get home and take her medicine."

Brandy walked back with Zoey. "Mom thinks everyone is nice."

"What if my dad likes Trudy? He called her neighborly."

"He called Erma family."

"Well, she kinda is. It's just that Trudy acts all gushy with me when Dad's around. When he leaves, she turns off all that sugar."

"You'll have J.J. around for two days. If Trudy brings a casserole, pretend J.J.'s staying longer. Pretend your dad really likes her."

Zoey brightened. "Good idea. Thanks. I'll call you later, Brandy. I'm excited that school's only a half day on Monday and then we're out till September."

Mack jumped out of the pickup and took the produce. "Honestly, Zoey, I told you Erma's in pain and we need to hurry home."

"Sorry." Zoey climbed unaided into the backseat.

"I'll take it as easy as I possibly can on the graveled section of our road, Erma. You seem like you're in even more pain now than when I took you to the doctor."

"The nurse said I don't have much padding over my old bones. She said to expect it to be bad for a week or two. I thought I was a tough old bird, but I hurt everywhere."

"I'm sure you tightened your muscles when you hit the cement. If it turns out you didn't chip or break a bone, it'll be pure luck." Mack soon left the smooth highway for a gravel track that led to the ranch. He slowed way down, but he could see tension building on Erma's face. The last thing Mack expected when he entered his circular drive was a strange SUV parked at his house. Did that mean Jill was still here?

Zoey squealed happily and unbuckled her seat belt

before Mack had completely stopped. "J.J.'s at the corral with Benny, Trevor and Eldon." Leaning into the front seat, Zoey pointed so her dad and Erma would look the right direction. "J.J. must like dogs. She's petting Jiggs."

Indeed, his herd dog, a two-year-old border collie, sat at Jill's feet, lapping up her attention. So did his foreman and wranglers. They were huddled around her, laughing and gesturing animatedly. A red haze of anger clouded Mack's vision. It wasn't until after he stepped out on his vehicle's running board and bellowed, "Since when doesn't time equal money on this ranch?" that he realized his irritation was due more to seeing Jill being lavished with attention from his wranglers than the fact his men were sloughing off work. He'd never been a hard-nosed boss.

HEARING THE BITE in Mack's voice, J.J. quickly scooped up her camera bag and gave the dog a last pat. She jogged across a patch of dry grass to his truck. "It's my fault the guys took a break," she said, squinting into the sun as she faced Mack. "When I arrived Benny was waiting for your veterinarian—you had a laboring cow in distress. The vet asked Benny to call your wranglers to hold the cow while she and Benny pulled the calf. I wanted to make sure everything turned out okay, so I stuck around. The whole process was worrisome but thrilling, especially when they got him. Once everything was okay, I took some candid shots of the work that goes on at your ranch. The fact that one of your cowboys is a former army sergeant will be great in my article on your charity work. Oh, hey, is that Erma you've brought home?"

J.J. lowered her voice as the woman in Mack's truck struggled to open the passenger door. "How is she?"

By then Benny and Jiggs the dog had crossed the yard from the corral.

"We had a cow in trouble?" Mack asked Benny. Stepping off the running board, he walked around the cab and reached for Erma to keep her from falling out the door. "Erma, you can't get out until I bring the wheelchair. Will someone please stay with her for a moment?"

J.J. rushed to comply, and Benny followed Mack to the rear of the pickup.

"Around noontime, Trevor stumbled across a young heifer set to deliver her first calf," Benny said. "He brought her to the barn because she seemed to be laboring too hard. We tried to help her, but she went berserk. She kicked me a good one on my shin. I called Delaney, who gave her something to calm her down."

Mack lifted the hospital wheelchair out and opened it, locking the seat in place. He listened to Benny with half an ear. The majority of his attention was focused on Erma exclaiming over how great it was to see Jill, and Jill responding with sympathy for Erma's plight.

"Benny, I'll take a look-see at the cow and calf after I get Erma inside. She needs to take her pain meds now."

Erma held on to her hip when Mack lifted her from the pickup and carefully set her in the wheelchair.

"I should have fixed that loose back step," Benny said sheepishly.

"I knew it was loose," Erma said as Mack wheeled her toward the house. "Accidents happen, Benny. Hey, did anyone gather the eggs? That's where I was headed when I fell."

Benny shook his head, so Mack said to Zoey, "Bug, you can gather eggs. Uh, sorry. I'm not going to have an easy time remembering you don't want to be called Bug."

"I hate gathering eggs, 'cause those old hens peck me."

"I've never gathered eggs," Jill said. "But maybe I can distract the chickens for you."

Erma waved a hand feebly. "Good idea. After you bring in the eggs, Jill, perhaps you can, uh, help me out of these clothes and into something more comfortable. These jeans are rubbing my sore hip."

Mack stopped at the base of the front porch steps. Anyone could see his displeasure.

"What's the matter, boss?" Benny eyed the makeshift ramp. "I cobbled boards together like you asked. Is there too much slope?"

"Huh? Oh, no. The ramp is fine. Jill is only here to do a job for her magazine, Erma. I believe she was headed back to town, weren't you?" He shot the query at their visitor.

Erma handed Mack the now-warm ice pack. "I'm really wobbly. I doubt Zoey has the strength to steady me and help me undress or dress. And that's definitely not a chore for you or Benny."

"I don't mind lending Erma a hand," Jill said.

Scowling at her, Mack said, "So, Benny, what's the verdict on your cousin? Can she get here right away?" Turning the wheelchair, he pulled Erma backward up the ramp and onto the porch.

"Sonja wants this job, but she can't get here till after next week. She's in Galveston taking care of her grandchildren while her oldest daughter and husband are on vacation. They left yesterday on one of those eight-day cruises to Mexico."

"Well that's a problem." Continuing to frown, Mack reached back to open the screen door.

Erma glanced over her shoulder at Mack. "Why's that? Seems to me we've got a solution. If Jill is taking pictures at the ranch, it makes sense for her to stay here instead of driving back and forth to town. I need a woman to assist me with private matters, like helping me in and out of the shower. I'm not a stork, you know. Can't stand on my one good leg."

"I'm pretty sure nursemaid isn't on Jill's professional résumé," Mack said. "Benny, I wish you'd phoned me about your cousin while I was still in town. I need to sign a contract with Leitha Davidson to find us someone even short-term." Mack's frustration couldn't be more obvious.

"Leitha won't go to all the work of hiring until Benny's cousin arrives," Erma stated firmly. "Jill's here. She said she's willing to help. Besides, I'm dying to hear all about Paris and where all else her work's taken her since she left Texas."

Zoey burst out, "J.J., you've been to Paris? That's so cool! Wait till I tell Brandy. Where else have you been?"

Mack bristled and interrupted before Jill could answer.

"Zoey, the eggs! You don't have time to hear how Jill gallivanted off to Paris and London and Rio and Tokyo..." He broke off, seeing Jill's eyes glitter, clearly curious about how he knew where she'd traveled. "I get the college alumni newsletter," he said. "They've mentioned you."

Jill nodded, but Erma didn't let up. "This house has four empty bedrooms, Mackenzie."

"Listen," Jill jumped in, spreading her hands. "I'm fine staying in town. I don't want to cause a family feud. If it's okay with you, Mack, I'll help Zoey gather the eggs, then settle Erma in. I'll come back tomorrow to begin our interview and take more photos."

Erma said something to Mack that J.J. couldn't hear. It served to make him duck his head and rub the lines creasing his forehead. A few seconds ticked by before he cleared his throat. "Erma's got a valid point. It's not like me to be inhospitable. I appreciate your willingness to help us out of a jam, Jill." Raising his head, he gazed squarely into her startled eyes. "Truly," he added. "My main concern should be doing what's best for Erma." He opened the door. "If you're okay with it, let's call a truce."

"Of c-course," J.J. stammered. "I'll just go put my camera bag away." She pointed to her SUV.

"Bring it in," Erma said. "Mackenzie means you should pick a bedroom and stay as long as you want. You and Zoey go collect the eggs while I take my pills. After you get me settled for a nap, you can check out of your motel. I wouldn't mind your help fixing meals for a few days."

Although she felt trapped, J.J. nodded. She wanted to bolt then and there—Mack couldn't have made clearer that he'd rather walk over spikes barefoot than have her stay at the ranch. Erma had to have twisted his arm, and who in their right mind would volunteer to be an unwanted houseguest?

"Awesome!" Zoey shouted. She dashed over to throw her arms around J.J.

From the porch, Mack watched Jill smile at Zoey and smooth her hands down the girl's braids. The simple, caring gesture hit him hard, chipping away some of the ice he'd built around his heart against Jill Walker. Her ready smile used to be something he loved. He vividly recalled the sweet taste of her lips, and unexpected heat moved through his groin. "So now that that's arranged," he muttered, "let's get this show on the road."

Benny said, "Don't forget, boss—we're planning to move the cattle to Monument Draw tomorrow. The summer range will make prettier pictures with the trees and all, but the herd's bound to kick up a passel of dust on the drive up there."

"Damn." With everything that had happened, Mack had forgotten. "Trailing the herd can mean a couple of days before any of us get back to the ranch."

"I have some extra days built in for this shoot," J.J. said. After all, Donna had urged her to spend an extra week visiting her mother. "I'll take a few pictures before you head out. Readers will like seeing you on a horse with a sea of steers as a backdrop."

"That would be a good plan except that we'll be leaving before daylight. It's a dry, hot drive between Turkey Creek and the next available water. The farther we get before sunrise, the better."

"Well, do whatever is necessary. I don't want to interfere. I'll keep Erma and Zoey company."

"I suppose we could delay the drive." Mack wasn't keen on the notion of leaving Zoey and an incapacitated Erma with Jill. The last time she was in his life, she hadn't thought twice about abandoning him. She probably wouldn't do that now, but she also didn't have any reason to stay. "There'll be time to figure this out at supper, which we won't have if we keep talking all day." He eased the wheels of Erma's chair over the threshold and disappeared inside.

J.J. worried her lower lip with her teeth as she followed Zoey to a row of chicken coops set away from the house in the shade of scrub oak. They were on a good-size plot, encompassed by a sturdy wire enclosure. "You have a lot of chickens," she said, pausing to latch the gate behind her.

"Erma uses a lot of eggs. Wait until you see how many Benny and Eldon eat at breakfast." Zoey unhooked one of the coop doors and exposed two shelves of nests, empty of chickens.

"So Erma cooks meals for the ranch hands as well as for your family?"

"We all eat together." Zoey reached into a nest and began placing eggs in one of her baskets. J.J. picked up a second basket and scooped the eggs out of the higher nests. They collected about twenty eggs, closed the coop and moved to the next. Hens were sitting on the nests in this one. One screeched and flew straight at J.J., pecking her arm.

"Ow!" She jumped back and dabbed at a trail of blood, trying to keep from dropping her basket.

Zoey unhooked a long-handled whisk broom off the inside wall of the coop and swatted the squawking hens. "Shoo." She flapped her arms at birds dive-bombing their legs. "We need to hurry and grab the eggs. The hens get braver the longer we stay."

J.J. filled her basket and topped off Zoey's while

the girl used the broom to keep the two most deter-mined hens away.

"Phew, that was a new experience for me," J.J. said as they dashed from the pen.

"You never kept chickens?" Zoey fastened the gate and took her full basket back from J.J.

"I went to college with a few ranch kids, but I lived on campus. And most of my friends lived in town. My stepdad was a math professor."

"You had a stepfather?" Zoey hesitated. "Was that okay?"

J.J. thought about how to answer. "It was fine. Un-like in your case, Zoey, my mom married Rex when I was a toddler. I never knew any other father."

Zoey hung her head. "I guess you read my essay, huh? I kind of hinted about wanting a mom."

J.J. wrinkled her nose and laughed. "That was more than hinting, Zoey. I'm guessing that's why you and Brandy didn't want your dad to read your contest entry at the library?"

"Yeah." She kicked a clod of dirt off the path. "I almost didn't mail it in. I figured anybody who read it would think I was nuts."

"Nope. The committee members were touched by what you wrote, but I should tell you, Zoey, if I'd been on the committee I would have voted no."

"Because you and my dad went to college to-gether?"

"No, because matchmaking is difficult to pull off. A one-time evening out… Well, I'm trying to say—don't get your hopes up, Zoey."

"Brandy's mom said I can't shop for a mother…" They reached the back door and Zoey trailed off.

Mack threw the screen open and stepped out onto the porch.

"Good, you're back. Erma's had her pills and she's already woozy." J.J. tried to sweep past him into the kitchen, but he grabbed her arm. "You're bleeding. What did you do?"

"A hen got her," Zoey announced matter-of-factly.

Mack pulled back his hand. "Wash that wound out. I'll grab the first aid kit. Chickens peck through all kinds of barnyard crap. I don't need your magazine suing me if you get blood poisoning."

J.J. rolled her eyes. "Your concern for my welfare is touching."

"I…" He sounded half rueful, half apologetic.

"Never mind," J.J. said, waving him off as she put her basket on the counter. She stuck her arm under the kitchen faucet and was drying it with a paper towel when Mack came back in. He was holding antibiotic cream and a plastic bandage. J.J.'s heartbeat quickened as he dabbed the cream onto her skin. Old feelings crowded in. Good and not so good, since this was the same kitchen where she'd stumbled upon him wiping away Faith's tears. Faith, who subsequently became his wife and Zoey's mother. Unwilling to deal with memories that still hurt, J.J. yanked back her arm. "That's good. Which way do I go to find Erma's room?"

Mack looked shaken by her hasty withdrawal. "Her room is where it's always been." He jerked his thumb toward the hall. J.J. did remember, now that she thought about it.

"Erma?" she called softly into the dark, silent room.

"Thank goodness," Erma said, sounding groggy. "I told Mackenzie to wheel me in here and go on about his business. But I desperately need to use the facilities. I tried to stand up but I got dizzy and fell back. Hurts even more now."

J.J.'s heart went out to the injured woman who'd always made her feel welcome here. Mack's father, too, had welcomed her. Jacob Bannerman had opened up to J.J., made her feel part of the family. He once admitted that his heart had broken permanently when his wife died. Another time he confided in her that the Bannermans were one-woman men. It was just as well that he didn't live to see his son make a liar out of him.

After she rolled Erma's wheelchair into the bathroom, J.J. slipped an arm around her and slowly lifted her. "Slide your left foot across the tile. Then if you can balance against the sink a moment, we'll get your jeans off."

"It's those danged pills making my whole body feel like limp spaghetti."

Indeed, J.J. felt as though she was grappling with wet noodles. It was a minor miracle that the two of them finally succeeded in getting the housekeeper out of her clothes. "Yikes, Erma! Your right side from your waist to your knee is a rainbow."

Erma barely nodded, but tensed as J.J. eased a nightgown over her head. Pain was etched on her face.

Giving Erma time alone, J.J. went out and fluffed the pillows. A few minutes later she helped her into bed.

"It's a good thing I sleep on my left side." Yawning, Erma sighed and her eyes drifted shut.

"Erma, I'm going to town to get my suitcases and check out of the motel. I won't be more than half an hour. Don't attempt to get out of bed on your own.

Zoey can stay nearby and find her father if you need anything."

"I'll be up to fix supper," Erma managed to say sleepily. "Mack and the men come in at six-thirty and expect to eat as soon as they sit down."

"So, what time do we have to start preparations?" J.J. asked, trying to read her watch in the darkened room. Silence greeted her query—Erma was already asleep. J.J. tiptoed out of the room.

Zoey was still at the kitchen counter brushing eggs and placing them in a covered container. "You were gone a long time. Is Erma okay?"

J.J. massaged a crick in her neck. "Her medicine really wiped her out. It was a challenge getting her into a nightgown." Then J.J. explained that Zoey had to listen in case Erma called out for help.

"What bedroom do you want, J.J.? My dad said to open it up and air it out. He said to check the bathroom for towels. We don't have many guests. The room next to mine upstairs is empty," Zoey offered.

Zoey clearly wanted J.J. to choose that one, but she said, "Is there a bedroom down here? Close enough so I'd hear if Erma needs help during the night?"

"There's one straight across the patio from her room. If you both left your doors open, I guess you could hear her through the screens."

"That's probably a better idea. I'll try to make it to town and back in half an hour. Erma fell asleep before I could find out what time we need to start supper. Poor Erma. Her side is so bruised I figure she'll need a lot of rest and help from us."

"I've never cooked anything," Zoey said. "Have you?" She sounded seriously concerned.

"We'll figure it out. We're capable of cooking, right, Zoey?"

"Oh, good. I heard my dad tell Benny there's no way someone who spends half her life hanging out with skinny models has the first idea of how to cook for a ranch crew."

That stung, but Mack hadn't been far off. Collecting her purse, she dug out her car keys. "There's some truth to your dad's statement, Zoey. I don't spend much time at home. If I host an occasional dinner party, I have it catered. All in all it's lucky Benny's cousin will be here soon." She winked at Zoey and left via the back door.

Chapter Four

Back in her motel room, J.J. repacked her bags. It was still early enough for her to phone her mother before she returned to the ranch. She hadn't yet gotten in touch with her mom, and she wanted to arrange a time to meet for lunch or dinner prior to her flight back to New York. Bonnie Walker's cell phone rang five times before she answered, sounding harried.

"Mom, it's J.J. I'm in Texas on a job."

"How nice, dear. But I can't talk now, I'm in my ceramics class."

"No worries. I'll be here for several days. Why don't I touch base tomorrow to set a time when we can do lunch or something?"

"All right, but my tai chi class starts at eight, then I have yoga until eleven. Oh, and my bridge group meets at my condo in the afternoon. Honey… I have to go. My vase is drying out."

"Uh—" Her cell went dead before she could say goodbye. She plopped down on the bed, not sure whether to be amused or irritated. It was typical of her mother, who was totally self-absorbed. And yet, four months earlier, her mom had acted depressed, convinced her life was in the toilet. The move to an assisted-living complex had obviously been good for her, worth every penny J.J. paid. A large part of Bonnie's concerns centered on money. J.J.'s stepdad's protracted illness had drained their savings. They'd borrowed against their home and when the market tanked the house was worth less than Bonnie owed, forcing her into a short sale. With her barely sixty and not eligible for social security, J.J. had stepped up to help financially, even though it meant delaying her dream of leaving her current job to freelance. She wanted to go after meatier stories, like poverty in American cities or the changing agricultural landscape.

J.J. felt weighed down and alone. Her life spun along a fast track in a business where it was difficult to make and keep friends, who often sped in opposite directions. What would it be like to settle down? She shouldn't envy women with loving husbands, who carpooled their kids around suburbia or lived in small towns like this one where the pace was way slower. But she did envy them.

Shaking herself out of her doldrums, J.J. pocketed her phone, rose and, out of habit, straightened the bedspread. She had to face hard truths when it came to her life. She didn't stay in one place long enough to develop a romantic relationship, and her ability to have children wouldn't last forever.

She went to the lobby and checked out, then stowed her bags in the SUV. She still wasn't sure bunking at Turkey Creek Ranch was a good idea. Her history with Mack left her on edge. Earlier when she'd driven down the ranch road for the first time in over thirteen years, she'd been assailed by memories. She'd once dreamed

of becoming his wife. She'd thought they would be
partners in every way. They'd made plans, ones that
evaporated in the blink of an eye that horrible evening she found out Mack had betrayed her—by getting his former girlfriend pregnant. In fact, the blow
had nearly crushed J.J. Her mother had urged her to
put Mack behind her, insisting she focus on her future.

Now, retracing the route to the ranch, she couldn't
stop wondering if he had made similar plans with
Faith. Mack had always said he wanted three children. Meeting Zoey was maybe what hurt the most.
J.J. had imagined having Mack's children. All at once
she found herself gripping the steering wheel too hard.

Relaxing her fingers, she forced her attention back
to the road. Covering old ground was pointless and
unhealthy. She should get rid of those old feelings.
So what if her life hadn't ended up the way she'd en-
visioned at twenty? She'd traveled to places others
longed to visit and met many interesting people. She
made an above-average living. She'd dated handsome,
well-connected men. Lamentably none ever measured
up to the high bar she had set for a husband. *Only
Mackenzie Bannerman had reached that bar, and then
he crashed into it.*

Darn! There he was, screwing with her mind again.
And he'd made it clear that he wasn't happy to see her.
She deliberately turned her thoughts away from him
to his daughter, and Zoey's poignant wish for her dad
to meet a woman and get married.

*As if that thought was going to drag her out of the
dumps.*

If she was honest, she'd admit that the very idea
of playing any part in helping find Mack a wife was

painful. She absolutely could not come back here in August to photograph him on his date with the magazine reader. She had to make Donna understand that.

The ranch house came into sight. J.J. reclaimed her spot between the house and barn. And she made herself a promise. She would get on with this assignment, treating it no differently than any of the others she'd handled over the years. Mack would be her job and nothing more.

Resolute, she hauled her suitcases up the makeshift ramp. She knocked, pushed open the door and called out. There had been a time she'd entered the house as if she belonged. This time she hesitated inside the foyer and called again, "Zoey? It's J.J. I'm back."

The girl bounded out of the kitchen. "Yay! Erma's still sleeping, but she usually fixes supper around now. What are we gonna do?"

"If you'll show me to my room, I'll drop my bags and go wake Erma."

"Okay." Zoey stepped through the archway. "This is the room I told you is directly across the patio from Erma's."

The room had white antique furniture, and the generous bed was covered with a dark blue spread. The thick pile carpet was gray. She had expected the same hardwood floors she remembered. The hardwood was still in Erma's room, thankfully, which made rolling her wheelchair easier.

"I wonder if Erma's doctor said anything to your dad about getting her a walker. She can't bear weight on her right leg, but in a few days she might be able to navigate better with a walker. They have front wheels that lock down. Erma could brace herself against the bathroom or kitchen cabinets, and probably wouldn't feel as helpless as she does relying on a wheelchair."

Zoey shrugged. "Dunno. But Benny and my dad fixed the back step while you were gone. Benny feels awful that he didn't do it the day Erma told him it was loose."

"I could tell he felt responsible. Zoey, can you set the table while I wake Erma and help her dress?"

Nodding, Zoey went to a freestanding buffet and hutch. J.J. entered Erma's room through the alcove and snapped on a lamp. The room flooded with light, but the woman on the bed didn't stir.

J.J. touched her shoulder. "Erma, I'm back." Erma's eyes flickered opened, but barely.

"We need to find you something comfortable to wear. Oh, a robe will work," J.J. said, spotting a cotton one looped over one bedpost.

Erma gazed vacantly at J.J., then closed her eyes again. J.J. tried a second time, but no luck. However much painkiller the doctor had prescribed, Erma seemed down for the immediate future.

Leaving the room, she propped the door ajar so they could hear Erma if she awakened.

"Where's Erma?" Zoey asked, rushing up to J.J.

"I'm afraid we're on our own fixing supper. Those pills zonked Erma out."

"Hoo boy!"

"Do you have any idea what she planned to cook this evening?"

"We bought stuff for a salad from Brandy's mom. My dad put it in the fridge. Oh, I remember Erma said she thawed hamburger to make meat loaf. Do you know what else goes in meat loaf?"

"No, but I can read a cookbook." She would normally look recipes up on her smartphone, but her data coverage was spotty in La Mesa.

Zoey nodded. "Erma has a whole shelf full of cookbooks." She pointed to a row of books standing upright between bookends made from horseshoes.

J.J. smiled at that as she did a quick reconnaissance of the kitchen. She realized she'd been wrong earlier. Mack's kitchen *had* been renovated. The cabinets were the same, but the appliances were new, stainless steel and big. The stove had six burners with a huge griddle in the center. The burners sat above double ovens. The refrigerator also looked industrial-size. It had side-by-side doors with a deep drawer at the bottom. An equally big upright freezer flanked the fridge on the other side.

"My dad loves chocolate cake," Zoey announced as she dogged J.J.'s footsteps. "He told Erma one time he'd be happy to eat cattle feed if he had chocolate cake for dessert."

"Then by all means, let's bake a cake. Uh, I hope Erma has cake mixes and doesn't whip hers up from scratch."

Zoey laughed and led J.J. across the room to a pantry that could pass for a mom-and-pop grocery store in New York City. Everything was lined up in order. J.J. selected a chocolate-chocolate cake mix, and a box of powdered sugar and dark cocoa for frosting.

"I'll get bowls," Zoey said, and ran to another cupboard. She pulled out two bowls and two round cake tins.

"Great, I'll mix this and put it in to bake if you'll set out salad stuff. And we need to find a meat loaf recipe." J.J. figured out how to preheat both ovens before she retrieved eggs from the fridge. She and Zoey worked in companionable silence for a while.

"Coffee," Zoey blurted as J.J. slid two cake pans into the oven. "My dad and the men drink gallons of coffee at every meal."

"No problem. I'll start coffee brewing and then tackle the meat loaf if you rinse the vegetables." She pulled carrots out of the fridge and a red onion. "We'll add these and our salad will be complete."

Zoey took the veggies to the sink. "Erma also does mashed potatoes and gravy whenever we have meat loaf."

J.J. closed her eyes and pressed the heel of one hand against her forehead. "That's a lot of food, but I suppose the men burn tons of calories chasing cows or whatever they do on the ranch. I think good gravy is an art."

Zoey didn't say anything.

"I know. I'll bake potatoes in the oven with the meat loaf. Will you scrub a dozen potatoes while I mix the meat loaf?"

"Sure. Cooking is hard, isn't it, J.J.? Erma makes it seem easy."

"It's probably like any job, Zoey. If you do something often enough it becomes second nature." J.J. cracked a few eggs over the ground beef. The oven timer dinged. She rinsed her hands, found mitts and removed two perfect-looking pans of chocolate cake—if she did say so herself. Sighing with relief she set them aside to cool.

"Oh, no! Zoey, you opened two cookbooks to meat loaf recipes but they're not alike at all. One calls for cracker crumbs, the other oatmeal. One uses tomato soup, the other tomato sauce. Any idea which Erma prefers?"

"I dunno." Zoey shook her head.

"I saw oatmeal in the pantry." J.J. hurried across the room. From the depths of the pantry she called, "I see canned tomatoes and salsa, but no tomato sauce or soup."

"Erma puts salsa on our enchiladas, and Benny pours it over his breakfast eggs. Soup isn't in the pantry. It's in the top cupboard next to the stove."

J.J. brought out oatmeal and the other ingredients. She lined them up on the counter, and took the time to look in on Erma again.

After she came back into the kitchen and unloaded the dishwasher, she dried her hands and said, "I think the cake is cool enough to turn out and frost. I'll do that now and finish the salad while the meat loaf cooks. By the way, the table looks perfect. But do you ever put candles on the table for ambience?"

"Erma has mason jars of candles we burn if we lose power and my dad is out with the cattle. When he gets home he starts the generator. What's ambience?" Zoey leaned her elbows on the counter.

J.J. laughed as she stirred up frosting from powdered sugar, cocoa and butter, and spread it over the bottom cake layer she'd turned onto a crystal platter she'd found in the hutch. "Ambience is creating a pleasant mood. If we put the men in a good mood they won't notice a few imperfections with the meal."

"That's smart. I'll get the candles. The potatoes are scrubbed."

Giving the top layer of the cake a final swipe with

the spatula, J.J. smiled with satisfaction and rinsed the empty frosting bowl. She poked holes in the potatoes before putting them in to bake, a trick she learned from her mom. She actually hummed while she measured dry ingredients to mix with the hamburger. "Where did you say I'd find tomato soup, Zoey?"

"The upper cupboard to the left of the stove."

J.J. pulled open the door and a can fell out. She grabbed for it, but missed. "Oh, no! No, no!" she yelped. "I can't believe it. My cake!"

Zoey ran out of the dining room. "What happened?"

"A can of chicken noodle soup fell out of the cupboard and made a huge crater in my beautiful cake." Gingerly, J.J. tugged out the buried can. The bottom was covered in frosting and cake crumbs. "I should have moved the cake to the center island."

"What a mess," Zoey said. It was obvious she was holding back a laugh. "Can you fix it?"

J.J. rinsed the can and set it on a paper towel. "I'm not sure." She moved the cake before another teetering can could fall and do more damage.

"You could fill the hole with frosting," Zoey suggested, rising on tiptoe to inspect the damage.

"That would be a sickening amount of chocolate even for a chocolate lover. I need to finish the meat loaf and get it in to cook, then toss the salad so at least the main meal will be done by the time your dad and the others come in. I'll try to repair the cake after."

"I'm sorry, J.J." Zoey gave her an impulsive hug.

"Thanks. I hope Erma feels well enough to supervise tomorrow. I'm out of my element, and I wanted this meal to be good to show your dad I'm not helpless." For a moment she rested her cheek atop Zoey's hair.

"You're great, J.J. I put four jar candles down the center of the table. Maybe I'll take away two. If it's darker in the dining room and if you cut the cake in here, I bet no one will notice. It'll still taste yummy."

J.J. laughed. "That's an excellent suggestion, kiddo. Just keep your fingers crossed that nothing else goes wrong."

Zoey grinned back. "I can't tear lettuce with my fingers crossed."

"Me, neither—I need two hands to work the soup and oatmeal into the hamburger."

"I liked meat loaf better before I found out what goes into it," Zoey said as they both returned to their chores.

A few minutes later, J.J. looked up. "This recipe calls for a whole can of tomato soup. I've poured in half a can and the mixture seems really juicy. I wonder how much hamburger Erma thawed. Maybe it wasn't as much as this recipe calls for. It says it serves a dozen."

"Counting you and me, there's only gonna be six of us. Seven if Erma wakes up."

J.J. studied the mixture. "We're short on time. The recipe suggests dividing the meat loaf into two pans for faster cooking." She shook her loose watch around her wrist to read it. "Erma said you eat at six-thirty. If I put this in the oven in two pans, it'll be done on time. So will the potatoes."

"Are you gonna make gravy?"

"No. I saw butter and sour cream in the fridge. That's better on baked potatoes." J.J. divided the meat mixture into two glass loaf pans and slid them into the oven. She poured the remaining soup down the drain.

"The lettuce is ready to go. Want me to put the dressing and stuff on the table?" Zoey asked.

"Please. And salt and pepper. Men love to pepper everything on their plates black and then turn it all white with salt."

"Benny does that. Daddy nags him."

"Hmm. Your dad's father died of a stroke. Salt drives up the blood pressure, and high blood pressure can lead to a stroke."

"I forgot until Erma and Daddy were talking about it today that his mom died of cancer when he was eight. I wish people didn't die."

J.J. glanced up from rinsing utensils. "It's hard for those left behind to make sense of death, Zoey. I lost a best girlfriend in high school. Gina Mahoney. She died in a water skiing accident. And in college a good friend, Tom Corbin, was killed on his motorcycle. We all had a hard time with his loss. He was your dad's friend, too."

"Erma said all living things have a season. And with people, some have short seasons and some have long ones. That doesn't seem fair."

J.J. didn't want to get into a deep philosophical discussion with Mack's daughter. She covered the salad. "The meat loaf is already starting to smell good. Listen, I'll go check on Erma, then we can see if any of those cookbooks have tips on repairing unplanned holes in layer cakes."

"It's kinda funny when you think about it," Zoey said, grinning.

"To you. But I was probably feeling too smug about how nice it turned out," J.J. agreed, sounding wry. "My mom always says pride goes before a fall."

"What does that mean?"

"It means don't get too full of yourself. Be right back." J.J. set the salad in the fridge as she headed for Erma's room.

"Erma." Bending down, J.J. shook the woman gently by the shoulder. "Supper will be ready in fifteen minutes. I doubt the doctor wants you to miss eating. Let me help you into the bathroom. You can wear your robe to supper."

Erma roused minimally. "I feel wrung out," she mumbled. "Give me ten more minutes to gather myself. Oh, mercy…did you cook?"

"With Zoey's help. Will you promise not to go back to sleep if I give you ten minutes? I baked a cake, but a soup can fell out of the cupboard and landed in the middle of it. I'll try to camouflage the damage, then I'll come back for you."

Erma eased up on one elbow. At the end of a long groan, she said, "The men like fruit. There are sliced strawberries in a green container in the fridge."

"Perfect. See you soon," J.J. said from the doorway.

"Is Erma okay?" Zoey asked.

"She needs ten minutes to pull herself together. She offered a solution for our cake problem." J.J. explained about the berries. "There's a lot you can learn from Erma, Zoey."

"About cooking." Zoey handed J.J. the berry container. "At school almost all the girls in my class have pierced ears," she said out of the blue. "In seventh grade girls wear skirts or dresses…and makeup. Erma only ever buys me jeans and plaid shirts. I don't want to hurt her feelings. That's a big reason why I sent your magazine that letter. I want my dad to meet and marry somebody who'll do mom stuff with me."

While she mixed strawberries with some ready-whipped cream she found in the fridge, J.J. considered Zoey's hazel eyes and reddish braids—totally unlike Mack's nearly black hair and smoky eyes. As she'd done earlier at the library, J.J. tried to picture Faith, whom she hadn't known well. She thought Faith had blue eyes and ash-toned hair. But either parent could certainly have had red hair in their backgrounds.

"What about your grandmother Adams?" J.J. asked. "Is she still around?"

"Yeah, but I don't see them much. They don't believe girls should ever cut their hair, or wear skirts that show their knees. I wore jeggings at Christmas, and Grandpa called them sinful." Zoey licked the spoon J.J. had set aside. "All my friends at school wear jeggings. I don't see what's sinful about them."

More memories came back to J.J. Faith's dad was a preacher of a very conservative church. Faith had defied them to attend Tech on a scholarship. Her parents had ordered her to turn it down to attend a bible college. Her refusal caused a huge rift. J.J. knew Mack had encouraged Faith's rebellion. *Maybe he'd had an ulterior motive.* But she couldn't think about that when, clearly, Zoey was asking her advice.

"Zoey, some teen girls go overboard with makeup and inappropriate clothes, trying to look older." She placed the repaired cake in the fridge. Turning, J.J. noticed the girl's crestfallen expression. "Hey, there's nothing wrong with looking fashionable, but not over-doing it. Maybe we can pick up a couple of teen magazines and find some outfits that would suit you and Brandy."

"Can we?" Zoey perked up. But the girl talk was cut short when the back door opened and the men tromped in.

"Zoey, I'll set the hot food on the table if you'll get the salad. Then I need to go help Erma."

Zoey dashed off, darting around her father, who said, "What's with the candles on the table? We haven't had a power outage."

"It's ambience, Daddy," Zoey said, brushing past him with the salad. "You'd better sit down. J.J.'s bringing the potatoes and meat loaf. And she has a surprise for dessert."

"A surprise? Where's Erma? Everything smells great, so I guess she's up to supervising."

J.J. transferred the baked potatoes to a basket and passed it across the island to Mack. "Here, make yourself useful as well as decorative."

That brought a ripple of laughter from the cowboys and Benny, who'd seated themselves at the trestle table. Even Mack snorted and smiled.

J.J. carried in first one pan of meat loaf and set it on a hot pad. Then she brought the second and took off her oven mitts. "Dig in. I'll go get Erma." She put a carving knife beside the dish closest to Eldon, one of the ranch hands. The meat loaf looked crustier than the picture in the recipe book, but, oh, well.

J.J. rushed into Erma's room in time to see the older woman trying to slide off the bed into the wheelchair. "Hold on, Erma, what are you doing? If you're going to try to get into the wheelchair, you need to push these levers first so it won't roll out from under you."

"I've always done for myself. I hate being laid up."

"I understand," J.J. said gently, "but we all need care occasionally. I see you managed to get your robe off the bedpost and put it on."

"I did, even though it hurt like the dickens."

J.J. straightened Erma's robe and helped her into the now-steady chair. "Do you need the bathroom before we go to the table?"

"Nope. Whatever you fixed smells delicious, but I'm afraid I'm not very hungry. Still, it's not often I get treated to a meal I didn't have to cook. Much as I nag Mackenzie to find a wife who'll share cooking and other household chores, he ignores me. Maybe now that you're back..."

J.J. broke in. "Not happening, Erma. I have a job on the other side of the country."

"Hmph. Well, the Lord works in mysterious ways."

As she wheeled Erma to the table, J.J. was aware that everyone suddenly fell silent, and the men all glanced down at their meals. Instead of slices of meat loaf, there were dark, unappetizing clumps on their plates.

"If nobody else is gonna tell Jill this meat's so dry we can't swallow it without ketchup, I will," Benny said, waving his fork. "Where's the ketchup?"

Aghast, J.J. left Erma at the table and she ran to get the large bottle of ketchup she'd seen in the fridge. "I'm s-sorry," she stammered, giving the bottle to Benny. "I've never made a meat loaf. There were two different recipes in Erma's books, and..." She broke off and sat down. With a pointed stare at Mack, she unfurled her napkin and said, "Since I hobnob with skinny models, you're all lucky I didn't serve you plain salad without dressing, or steamed tofu." Mack and Benny both had the grace to look guilty.

Then Mack's eyes crinkled at the corners and he laughed. "I deserve that, Jill. I thought you were out of hearing range when I made that comment to Benny. It was uncalled for and I'm sorry. And this meal is fine, considering the guys and I will be eating cold beans and dry biscuits for the next couple of days while we move the herd."

"Dang right, so pass the ketchup," Trevor said, after which the men's talk turned to the gear they'd need to assemble for the trail drive.

The food disappeared and Erma began to nod off. Jerking awake, she cleared her throat. "Save the cow talk until after dessert. I want some of Jill's cake before I head back to bed."

"You baked a cake?" Mack sounded pleased.

Sliding out of her chair, J.J. said, "Mack, you pour coffee all around. Zoey, I'll cut the cake if you'll carry the slices from the kitchen."

The girl jumped up at once. Jill cut generous slices of cake, taking care to spoon berries and cream over the ragged inner edges.

"Chocolate," Mack exclaimed. "Erma, did you tell her that was my favorite?"

"I didn't tell her anything. I intended to get up and oversee things, but I'm afraid those painkillers left poor Jill and Zoey on their own."

This time when Mack looked at Jill, his smile glowed warmly.

She nodded to his daughter. "Zoey deserves more than half the credit. Without her valuable input I would've been sunk. My meat loaf wasn't the only disaster. This two-in-one dessert is because—"

"Shh." Zoey waved a hand in front of J.J.'s face. "The way you fixed it, nobody has to know."

"Now they really have to know," J.J. said, looping her arm over Zoey's shoulders. "A can of soup fell out of the cupboard and dive-bombed dead center in my freshly frosted cake."

After his first bite, Mack said, "I agree with Zoey, you didn't need to tell us. It tastes great."

Erma motioned J.J. and Zoey back to the table. "The number-one cook's rule—what happens in the kitchen, stays in the kitchen."

Everyone laughed at that, and J.J. finally felt her stomach relax. Until the men finished and trooped out, and Erma asked to go back to her room and Zoey bounded past saying, "I need to call Brandy."

J.J. settled Erma. She wrote her cell number on a piece of paper and tucked it beneath Erma's bedside phone. "I'm in the room directly across the patio. If you need me for anything at all during the night, holler out and I'll be there."

The older woman squeezed J.J.'s hand. "Say all you want that your place is in New York. Tonight this family felt whole for the first time in years. Mackenzie and Zoey felt it, too. Yessireebob." Smiling softly, Erma sank down on her pillow.

The very idea sent squiggles of tension through J.J. As she returned to an empty kitchen and faced cleanup alone, Erma's words stoked old yearnings J.J. tried to deny. Ignoring the melancholy feelings, she dived in, rinsed plates, stored a few leftovers and fed what remained of the very dry meat loaf to Jiggs. The dog lapped it up without ketchup or complaint.

It was after nine by the time she set the last pan in the dishwasher. The house had grown quiet. J.J. assumed Zoey had a nightly routine. Mack, she supposed, subscribed to the early-to-bed-early-to-rise custom of most ranchers. For someone who still ought to be on East Coast time, she wasn't sleepy. She recalled seeing a bottle of white wine in the fridge. Getting out a glass, she poured some and retired to her room.

J.J. wandered to the open French doors, where the balmy night drew her onto the patio. A few small lanterns around the perimeter of the swimming pool added to the burnished glow from a golden moon. The faint light outlined a lawn swing that beckoned her. Sitting, she started it swinging, then tucked her legs up on the seat. J.J. sipped her wine as she searched for constellations in the star-studded night sky that she rarely saw in New York.

The sound of footsteps on the flagstones caused her to jump, almost spilling her wine.

"Sit," Mack said. "I saw you from my room." He pointed to another door that opened onto the pool. "I wanted to apologize."

J.J.'s heart sped up and her breath caught in her throat as Mack came closer. Was he finally going to tell her he was sorry for the shabby way he and Faith had treated her? Her fingers tightened around the cool glass. She was ready to hear it and act magnanimous.

"I do my best to set a good example for Zoey. Today when I criticized you to Benny for no reason I wasn't a good role model. So, forgive me, Jilly."

It took her a moment to realize she and Mack were on different wavelengths. "You already said you were sorry at supper. Anyway, it was no big deal."

"Tonight you cooked, entertained Zoey and looked after Erma. I'm grateful."

She wrapped her free arm around her waist. J.J. didn't want Mack seeing any sign of nerves. "I feel bad for Erma. For all of you."

He reached out as if to touch her, then dropped his hand. "I think I'm still in shock from seeing you in town, and then working in my kitchen. You haven't changed." His voice fell to a husky whisper. "It's as if those years since college didn't happen." He moved closer and J.J. felt each word travel up her spine as she set her wine glass on the wooden arm of the swing. She loosened her other hand from around her waist and held it out to maintain a distance, but it was too late. Her hand collided with his chest, her icy fingers welcoming the warmth.

"Jilly…" Mack bent his head.

Her brain screamed a warning, telling her to retreat. But she was held prisoner by his smoky gaze. She licked her lips and tasted the oak from the chardonnay. Then he crushed her against his hard lean body and kissed her, and kissed her and kept kissing her until Mack was all she tasted.

Her arms—in fact, her entire body—went pliant.

Only after Mack tightened his hold on her waist and abruptly stepped away from her did J.J. realize her glass had tipped over, spilling the wine onto the swing. Her pleasure diminished when she saw the pain and regret in Mack's eyes, at odds with his unfair accusation when he said, "Stop. Stop being so tempting, dammit!" He frowned and added, "You can't turn back the clock. Don't even try, Jill." Wheeling, he strode toward the open door.

"Me?" she sputtered. "*You* kissed *me,* you jerk!"

His door slammed shut and sent a jolt to her toes. She lost track of how long she stood in a puddle of moonlight before she collected her empty glass, listening to crickets chirp—three fingers pressed against her lips as she tried desperately to hang on to Mack's kiss.

Chapter Five

Mack sat on his bed and cradled his head in his hands. Kissing Jill had been stupid, stupid, stupid. Seeing her on his patio in the moonlight had made the years dissolve. Once, their love had been strong. Her abrupt departure had stunted his capacity to trust—trust his ability to make sound judgments when it came to love and women. He should have refused when Erma wanted her to stay. From the moment he saw her at that table in the library, his life had teetered like a seesaw.

Maybe Erma had been right. Maybe he needed a woman in his bed—in his life. But not Jill. Her very presence sparked too many painful memories. It was a good thing he was leaving early in the morning. It'd give him a couple of days to get his head on straight enough that he could be in the same room as Jill without fighting the urge to kiss her.

THE REST OF the night proved to be restless for J.J. Afraid she would miss hearing Erma should she call, or not call because she didn't want to be a bother, J.J. tiptoed into the housekeeper's room at midnight and again at 2:00 a.m. Both times she found Erma sleeping without a twitch. J.J. was glad to see she was breathing regularly and showed no signs of pain. Regardless, each time she returned to her room J.J. tossed and turned or stared at the ceiling, wide-awake—reliving that sizzling kiss.

Shortly before four she managed to drift off but awoke to a strident buzzing that seemed to come from outside. Distantly she heard Erma calling her. Because she hadn't fully undressed for bed J.J. simply yanked on her boots and raced across the patio. Her heart hammered. What if Erma had fallen again?

"My alarm is going off and I can't reach it." Erma waved an arm toward a nightstand on the other side of her bed. It was still dark outside, and she'd switched on a bedside lamp.

J.J. hit a few buttons on the clock before one finally silenced the noise.

Erma attempted to sit up. "It's time I started breakfast for Mack and the hands." She'd barely finished her statement than she fell back on the pillow with a groan. "Those danged pills are messing with my old bones. The doctor said to take the pills exactly as directed on the bottle. All they do is make me worthless."

J.J. eased Erma into a sitting position. "Does this hurt?"

Erma nodded. "Maybe not as much as yesterday. Will you help me hop into the bathroom?"

"Hopping will jar your hip. The wheelchair's at the end of your bed. Let me wheel you in. I'll dampen a washcloth with warm water and get you a towel, then go start coffee before I come back for you. A sponge bath should help you feel more human. Mack said the doctor wants you to rest, but I wonder if those pills are too potent. After breakfast let's call and ask if you can reduce the dose."

Erma nodded. She slid out of bed and stood on her good leg, but the minute she touched her right foot to the floor, her leg buckled and she cried out in pain.

J.J. grabbed her and braced her so she didn't fall, then moved the wheelchair into place.

"What kind of pain pills only work when I lie down?" Erma complained.

"Injured muscle and bones don't heal overnight." J.J. got the older woman into the chair and wheeled her into the bath. "Are you steady enough for me to leave you alone for a few minutes?" she asked after she wet a washcloth.

Erma made shooing motions with the hand not holding the cloth she'd accepted. "Did I dream it, or did Mack say they're trailing the herd to Monument Draw today? If so, he and the men need a hearty breakfast, plus extra biscuits to take along. And canned beans."

"According to Zoey the men eat a lot of eggs every morning. I hope they like them scrambled, because mine always turn out that way."

"That crew scarfs 'em down any way I cook 'em. Benny and Eldon pour an inch of salsa over everything on their plates, anyway." Erma snickered. J.J. responded with a smile, feeling better about leaving Erma to her own devices while she went to brew coffee.

J.J. shuffled into the kitchen. Thankfully she remembered where the coffee was stored. Feeling sluggish after her own sketchy sleep, she made the coffee stronger than the previous evening's.

Yawning, she emptied the dishwasher and quickly

set the table. The smell of fresh coffee made her mouth water. She turned from the table to pour a cup for herself and Erma, and ran right into Mack, who was backing out of the pantry. He held two loaves of store-bought bread in one hand. The other he put out to steady J.J.

She blinked, partly from the force of the impact, partly due to how he looked. Today he wore snug, scruffy blue jeans rucked up over black, square-toed boots. His blue shirt hung open, giving her a peek at his suntanned chest. J.J. swallowed. Mack hadn't shaved and the rough-hewn cowboy look had never been more appealing. Trying to calm her racing heart, she couldn't help hoping his unkempt appearance was because he'd spent as sleepless a night as she had after their kiss.

"What are you doing up so early? I figured you'd sleep in."

"Why? Because someone kept me up late…hmm?"

"Uh, Jill, about last night…" Looking abashed, Mack cleared his throat.

Still stung from the way he'd hightailed it after kissing her the way he had, J.J. hunched, and stepped around him. "Last night was moon madness. Forget it, Mack. I have."

Seeming relieved, he surveyed the kitchen. "Where's Erma?"

"In the bathroom. Her alarm woke us both at four." Taking two ceramic mugs off the counter, J.J. stopped by the percolating coffeemaker. "I'll bring some coffee to her and see if that chases away her cobwebs. Those pain pills wipe her out. Out of curiosity…what are you doing with the bread? Erma said you'd want eggs and biscuits, with extra to take on your trip."

"I thought we'd have toast and eggs. Unless you're offering to whip up biscuits?" he said with a hopeful lilt.

"You mean biscuits that aren't as dry as my meat loaf?" J.J. couldn't help her cutting tone. Even if incompetent was the last way she wanted him to think of her.

Mack watched Jill pour liberal amounts of cream and sugar in her coffee. It made him smile in spite of himself. Really, very little seemed to have changed about Jill—except she'd grown even prettier. As she rested the spoon on the counter and picked up both mugs, he was struck by how right it felt to see her in his kitchen. But sudden anguish washed over him. Again he wondered why she'd taken off all those years ago with no explanation. The last time they had spoken, he'd dropped out of college to run the ranch, and he'd assumed they'd make a life together. *Was this current show of compassion all for her magazine?*

He still hadn't read what Zoey had written about him. He thought about her babbling outside the library. What had she said about getting picked? That someone—a woman—would deliver a check for his charity? And she kept mentioning a date. That part ran together with someone saying she looked like a boy. Mack frowned, unable to connect that. With Zoey's button nose, scattered freckles and pretty rust-colored braids, she looked like a girl to him.

"Jill," he blurted, catching her a moment before she headed back to Erma's room, "How does Zoey strike you?"

His question stopped her. "From the little time I spent with her, she seems like a sweet, polite kid. Why?"

"No special reason. It used to be that whenever she wasn't at school she was my shadow." A smile briefly played across his lips. "This past year she's shown less interest in what's happening around the ranch. She mopes around inside a lot."

J.J. juggled the hot mugs and debated how much to involve herself in Mack's and his daughter's lives. She considered saying nothing, but would he have asked her advice if he wasn't bewildered? And her being here had come about because Zoey was concerned for her dad's happiness, and her own future. J.J. decided to offer an opinion. "Mack, Zoey's almost a teen. For a girl, that transition's comparable to a caterpillar becoming a butterfly."

"Huh?" Mack set the loaves of bread on the counter and ran a hand over his stubbled jaw. "You mean... like growing pains? I had those as a boy." He buttoned his shirt and tucked it in his jeans.

She pursed her lips. "I don't know about growing boys, but the teenage years can be awkward for a girl who sees changes in her friends and not in herself."

"You, uh, mean like getting, uh, breasts?" Mack gestured with his hands, but his face turned red.

J.J. found his discomfort endearing. "There may be some anxiety about that, yeah, but by and large with girls it's more emotional. Some navigate this stage easier than others. Excuse me, Mack, maybe we can talk about this later. I need to help Erma." J.J. left him looking perplexed, and hoped she hadn't muddied the waters too badly. But she knew that she wasn't the right person to help Zoey Bannerman get her heart's desire—a mother. Lordy, now that she'd opened her mouth, she might be stuck trying to tell Mack that he needed to find a wife. *Impossible!*

She might have been able to let go of the past— if Mack hadn't kissed her last night. It clearly hadn't affected him the way it did her. For J.J. the kiss had brought back their shared dreams. Coming here, spending the day in Mack's home, had dredged up memories of a time she'd valued. He'd probably been bombarded with guilt over what he'd done.

She thought she'd convinced herself that her career was enough—that she didn't need a man to fulfill her. Kissing Mack had caused doubts. So, the minute he returned from moving his cattle, she'd take the required photographs and get out of here. Get away from Mack.

"Erma, I brought coffee," she sang out, forcing herself to sound lighthearted. "I hope you still like yours with a splash of cream."

"I can't believe you'd remember such a trivial thing about me, considering how long ago you took off to make your mark on the world." Erma, in her wheelchair, accepted the mug. Her observation came with a raised eyebrow that J.J. sensed was a request for an explanation. Erma wanted to know why she'd flown from Texas, but J.J. didn't feel she ought to talk about it. If Mack hadn't explained their breakup, why should she?

Erma doted on Mack. So if he'd kept her in the dark about his deceitful ways, J.J. wasn't about to enlighten her. "Photographers pay attention to detail," she said, glossing over Erma's veiled question. "I'll put our mugs here and find you some clothes. What would you like?"

"It's supposed to be hot again. I have lightweight gray sweatpants in my top dresser drawer. They'll be loose on my bad hip. There should be a T-shirt in the closet."

"Sounds good."

They spent the next several minutes trading Erma's nightwear for sweats.

"Wow, your bruises are even more colorful today," J.J. said, taking care when she slid the sweatpants over Erma's hips.

"Moving hurts like the devil. Up to now I've never been sick a day in my life."

"You're not sick, which is why you're so impatient." J.J. found it easier to help Erma into a roomy red T-shirt. "Where's your brush? A big plus is that your hair is naturally curly."

"Thank the Lord for small favors." She opened a drawer in the bathroom vanity and swept a brush through her iron-gray hair a few times. "I feel better, thanks to you, Jill." Erma reached for her coffee. "A few more swallows of this and I can help out with breakfast."

"Get a good grip on your mug before I wheel you to the kitchen. Mack's already there. He intends to serve Benny and the guys toast and eggs. After my meat loaf, I think he's afraid I'd make hockey-puck biscuits. I'd never admit it to him, Erma, but between us, I've only ever baked biscuits that come from a can."

"Stick with me, girl. You'll be a ranch cook in no time," Erma said as they rounded the corner.

"Jill's not going to be here that long." Mack rose

from where he knelt pouring kibble in Jiggs's bowl. The dog rushed in to eat. "You look cheerier today, Erma," Mack said. "I hope you feel better."

She made a face at him. "The pain is tolerable. Even so, don't you be running Jill off. I've been telling you that you need someone just like her—a woman with vigor and vitality."

J.J. hushed Erma by suddenly sliding a bread-board across the arms of her wheelchair. "Tell me what you need for biscuits. I'll set you up, then fire up the griddle and scramble some eggs. Will Zoey be down soon?" J.J. asked Mack. "If so, maybe she can pour everyone orange juice."

"Lately Zoey's not an early bird," he said. "I'll pour the juice. What about fruit, Erma? Do we have any to put out?"

"There's canned peaches and pears in the pantry. Open whichever you want. And get out black beans to go along with leftover biscuits for your ride." Bending to the side, Erma winced, but still retrieved a bowl from a lower cabinet, along with cookie sheets. She handed both to J.J., who rushed to assist her.

"So, you're going on horseback?" J.J. was surprised. "I assumed you'd drive."

"That's city-girl thinking," he said with a wink at Erma. Turning back to J.J., he asked, "Have you even seen a horse since you left Texas, let alone ridden one?"

"I have." J.J. frowned in indignation, then shrugged. "Okay, rarely. I rode in Italy and a couple of times on other remote shoots." She passed Erma the ingredients she requested, and a fork to stir with.

"Hmm, we may have to cancel having you take

pictures of me with the herd," Mack said, pausing as he dumped pears into a bowl. "I thought once the cattle were calm, you and I could ride out to the draw and back in one day. But if you haven't ridden in a while, you'd end up too saddle-sore to sit for a cross-country flight."

"Don't sell me short," J.J. said, further irritated because the sight of his large hands around the can made her insides squirm. "Magazine photography isn't all glamour. I've trekked into some wild and woolly spots, and I always carry my own equipment."

"Touchy, I see," Mack drawled.

"You're darned tootin'." She tossed back some of the Texas lingo she hadn't fully lost. "I'm no hothouse flower, Mack. If I wasn't needed here today, I'd ride along and photograph your whole trail ride. And I wouldn't need special privileges."

"If it bothers you to stay behind with Zoey and Erma," he snapped, "I'll leave the guys to calm the herd and ride back here this afternoon."

"I'm not bothered." She drew back, giving him a puzzled look. "Are *you* bothered about leaving me here? Are you afraid I'll run off with the Bannerman silver?" Cracking the eggs, she stirred them vigorously, then stared at Mack, who remained silent. *Of all the nerve.* She wasn't the one who'd broken their trust.

"What's with you two carping at each other like a couple of caged bobcats? Of course we three will be fine," Erma said huffily. "Jill, would you hand me an egg, salt, cream of tartar and the milk? And then, please preheat the oven to four hundred and fifty."

After glaring at Mack again, J.J. got the ingredients. "You make mixing biscuits look so easy, Erma."

"This is my grandmother's recipe. I've been making these drop biscuits almost from the time I learned to walk."

Mack laughed. "You told Trevor you were six when you first made them. Next time you tell the story you'll have come out of your mama's womb making biscuits."

"Smarty pants. Point is, I've made this recipe so often I could make them in the dark."

"And they're always good," he said. "Jill, you don't cook?"

"I'm not home long enough at any one stretch," J.J. said. "I cooked when I was younger, even though my mom used to say the only reason we had a kitchen was because it came with the house."

"How are your folks?" Mack asked, his voice a rumble from across the room.

"It's just Mom now. Rex died last fall."

Mack stepped up to the counter. "I'm sorry. I didn't know. Is Bonnie still in Lubbock?"

J.J. nodded. "I found her a condo in a nice retirement village. At first she was a basket case, but that's all changed. I spoke to her yesterday and her calendar is so full I'm not sure she'll be able to fit me in for a visit."

She'd delivered the information with a smile, but Mack sensed an underlying hurt. Bonnie Walker had always been selfish, and Jill was often an afterthought. A lesser person would have written her mother off. In fact, the day his ring arrived in the mail, he'd called Bonnie. She'd said Jill jumped at a marvelous opportunity. In the following days, rumors circulated among their friends that Jill had chosen a career over marriage.

He was on the verge of demanding she 'fess up herself, but Benny and the men trooped in and brought him back to earth. Benny and Erma knew some of his history with Jill. But to Eldon and Trevor, nothing was sacred. The way Jill dumped him had left Mack skittish, and he'd rather they didn't know. He didn't need their teasing.

Within minutes everyone sat at the table. The room fell silent as they all tucked in. The crew polished off their breakfast in fewer minutes than it had taken to prepare. Then the men said goodbye and departed.

"It's time for another round of pain pills," Erma said, shifting in her chair to ease her sore hip. "Jill, will you pack up the leftover biscuits for the men?"

"Okay. Erma, do you want the full dosage?"

"Yes. I'm ready to go lie down."

J.J. got the bottle and shook out two tablets. "With nothing going on here today, you can sleep until noon. Extra rest will probably do you good."

"There're eggs to gather," Erma fretted. "The men won't take all the horses, so they'll need to be fed. And it's wash day. But I suppose that can wait."

Mack came in the back door in time to hear Erma. "I fed the horses. Zoey can feed the chickens and pick up eggs. The wash…" He shook his head. "That's too much to ask you to do for my family." He hung his straw cowboy hat on a rack by the door.

"I'm quite able to do the laundry, Mack."

"Absolutely," Erma said, glowering at him. "As far as the wash goes, though, we need to conserve water due to the drought. We should wash clothes less often."

"How bad is the drought?" J.J. asked. "I heard some men discussing it at the café in town. That's why I questioned whether you'd hold your charity event,

Mack. One of the men said you might have to sell some cattle early because of the water shortage."

"I wondered what prompted that remark. It's toughest on the ranchers who run free-range cattle. I lease summer grazing in the high desert where water is a bit more plentiful. And thanks to Turkey Creek, our wells aren't dry. But the short answer is drought is never good if you're in the business of ranching."

J.J. nodded. "I shouldn't have run the dishwasher last night. With just the three of us here while you're away, we'll stack our breakfast and lunch dishes and wash them with our supper dishes."

"Now you're thinking like a West Texan." Mack grinned.

J.J. sniffed regally.

"I'm, uh, going to run up and tell Zoey so long," he said abruptly. "I'll try to get home today, but if I don't show up by suppertime, eat without me."

"Could you give us a ring and let us know?" J.J. asked, pausing as she wheeled Erma into the alcove. "So we can cook the right amount."

"Cell service is sketchy, as you know. But I'll try." Mack turned and started down the hall.

"Oh, Mack," J.J. called belatedly. "If we find ourselves with time to kill, would you mind if I take some photographs of Zoey? She seems to believe that other girls her age are…cuter. I'm sure they're not. But professional equipment does wonders to bring out a subject's best features. I thought I could take a few photos and maybe use your printer later so Zoey can see herself the way other people do."

Mack frowned throughout her explanation and J.J.

expected him to refuse. She was pleasantly surprised when he removed the hat he'd grabbed from the rack, slapped it on his thigh and said, "Zoey never likes her school pictures. If anyone can take a photo she'll like, it'd be you, Jilly."

She nodded and continued toward Erma's room.

"Hey," he shouted after her, "you won't dress her up like one of those kid models on TV, will you?"

"I'd never do that." She leaned around the wall and hoped Mack saw her sincerity. His remark dented her anticipation at working with Zoey. Mack didn't trust her, and she honestly didn't understand why. She wasn't the one who broke promises—and hearts.

"I happen to think she looks fine as she is…" Mack's voice trailed off.

J.J., who knew Zoey didn't feel she was up to par with other girls in her class, wondered if she should have shared that with Mack. She worried she was getting in deeper with this family than was wise.

Erma didn't comment one way or the other, and once in her room she declined to change into sleepwear. "I'll nap a while and hopefully by lunch I'll feel like joining you and Zoey."

J.J. assisted Erma into bed. She covered her with a light blanket and turned on the overhead fan. "If you need anything while Zoey and I are doing chores outside, you have my phone number. I'll check on you often. I'd like to do some of those photos of Zoey indoors, and some outside."

"You spending time with Zoey will be good for her," Erma said. "I love that little monkey to pieces, but kids today aren't like kids were when I grew up. The whole world is different. I see that every time I turn on the TV. Zoey was a happy child. Now she acts like she's carrying around a weight." Erma yawned. "For years I've been telling Mack that girl needs a mother. What do *you* think? I say a young man and an old woman raising a girl from infancy is like trying to load frogs in a wheelbarrow."

J.J. laughed in spite of herself. She wasn't about to give an opinion on Mack's marrying again. "From the little I've seen, you shouldn't be so hard on yourself and Mack."

Erma burrowed into the pillow and closed her eyes. "Mack says the same thing. Only he says I should stop meddling in his love life. I reckon if he had a love life I'd stay out of it." She sighed and fell silent.

Expecting more, J.J. waited. But Erma had fallen asleep, so J.J. slipped out of the room. She got to work clearing the kitchen table.

"There you are," Mack said, sauntering in from the hallway. He removed his battered straw hat and fiddled nervously with the rolled brim. "I told Zoey you asked to take her picture. She shot out of bed quicker than I've seen her do in ages. She'll be down shortly, but I told her chores come first." Mack put on his hat again. "I, uh, decided I won't break my neck getting back tonight. More than likely, Benny and I will ride in around noontime tomorrow if that's okay with you."

J.J. glanced up sharply from the stack of plates she carried to the counter. "It's your call, Mack. All I'm doing is hanging around until you slow down enough for me to do the job I was sent to do." She passed him two bags of biscuits and the canned beans.

Taking them, Mack said, "Nevertheless, you're

doing me a huge favor when you certainly have no reason to put yourself out for me and my family."

His cool insinuation that nothing personal remained that could allow for friendship cut deep into J.J.'s heart. She wanted to ask why things had gone so wrong between them, but the clip-clop of horses outside, along with Benny shouting Mack's name, stopped her.

"I have to go," he said. "By the way, Delaney will drop by the barn later. She may or may not stop at the house."

"Delaney?" J.J. had heard the name, but couldn't place where.

"Dr. Blair, our vet." Mack opened the door and stepped out onto the back porch.

J.J. followed and saw him put the food in leather saddlebags before he swung into the saddle in one easy, fluid motion that did funny things to her stomach. Darn, but he looked good sitting tall astride a powerful black horse. Maybe because she'd been born and raised a Texan, seeing a man on a horse affected her equilibrium far more than men in three-piece suits striding purposefully down Madison Avenue.

Benny tipped his battered hat to her. Mack did the same before sending his mount off at a trot. He flashed J.J. a smile that left her even weaker in the knees. She stood in the doorway until the men rounded the barn and disappeared from sight. She might not have gone inside had Zoey not bounded out shouting her name.

"Well, good morning. Your dad just headed out. Yesterday he said they'd leave when it was still dark, but look—there's a beautiful orange sunrise beginning to streak the sky."

Zoey pranced around on tiptoe. "Daddy said Eldon and Trevor left earlier with the herd. And he said you wanted to take pictures of me! I wish Brandy could come over so you could take some of her, too. But I talked to her last night and she has to help her mom pick vegetables today. This weekend she's working to earn half the price of a leather jacket she saw at Dillard's in Lubbock. It's so cool. But she's gonna miss spending today with you. That's better than any leather jacket."

"We have chores to do first, Zoey. Do you get paid for feeding the chickens and gathering eggs? If so, you can save up for your own jacket."

Zoey's demeanor changed once they returned to the kitchen. "My dad doesn't believe in paying me to do chores. He says I should help out because it's the Bannerman ranch and I'm a Bannerman. He has a whole lecture about profits going toward everything we do, like what we eat and wear and stuff."

"Hmm. So how does it work if, say, you wanted a jacket like Brandy's saving up for?"

Zoey's shoulders sagged. "How it works is Erma has a household account at the bank, and a charge account in town at the general store. She buys my clothes there. Blue jeans and plaid flannel shirts is all they have."

"I see. Shall we go feed the chickens? Maybe giving them corn will distract them so we can gather the eggs before they peck us."

Without complaint Zoey carried the baskets. At the coops, she returned to the subject. "Erma doesn't drive as much as she used to. Otherwise, maybe we'd go to Lubbock to shop once in a while."

"Have you brought this up with your dad?"

Zoey shook her head. "I'm afraid to say anything. There's this woman in La Mesa, Trudy Thorne— Well, you heard Dad talking to her on the phone at the library. She's always flirting with him, but if he's not around she's not very nice to me. And she's really not nice to Erma."

"Oh?"

"No one knows except Brandy, but one day I heard Trudy tell Brandy's mom that if Dad opens his eyes and sees Erma's getting too old to be our housekeeper, he'll fire her. Then Trudy will show him *she's* indis... pensible." Zoey stumbled over the word. "I don't think he will, 'cause yesterday driving home he told Erma she's family. All the same, if he knew I hate the clothes she picks out for me, he might say something in town, and Trudy would start hanging around the ranch."

J.J. followed the story in silence, quickly collecting eggs while Zoey scattered cracked corn. She'd never met Trudy Thorne, but she knew unequivocally that she wouldn't warm to the woman. Only an ogre wouldn't like Zoey and Erma. Surely Mack had the sense to see that someone making a play for him wasn't sincere about his daughter. On the other hand, J.J. had seen men dazzled by some women's coquettish nonsense.

They exited the chicken pen, J.J. pondering how she might put a bug in Mack's ear when an older SUV pulled up to the barn.

Zoey erupted excitedly, handed J.J. her full egg basket and took off running toward the flame-haired woman exiting the vehicle.

J.J. realized this must be the veterinarian who had delivered the distressed cow's calf the previous afternoon. She had been so caught up in the cow's horrific situation, she hadn't really looked at the vet. Today, as Dr. Blair ambled toward them, J.J. studied the very attractive woman who was close to her own age. Zoey was hugging the woman, and when J.J. got within earshot, she heard the girl ask the whereabouts of someone named Nick.

The vet retrieved a medical bag out of her pickup bed. "He's running a fever, Zoey. I left him with his sitter."

J.J. noticed an identifiable anxiety puckering the space between the woman's eyebrows. Nearer now, J.J. saw how slender the vet was. Probably a lot of people found her fragile appearance incongruent with her job—as did many people who saw J.J. packing her equipment for a remote shoot.

"Hi," J.J. said, setting down both egg baskets to extend her hand. "We sort of met yesterday, but you were busy with a patient. I hope the heifer is better today."

"So do I. It was touch and go when it came to saving her and the calf." Delaney Blair shifted her heavy bag to her left hand and extended her right for J.J. to shake. She noticed that the vet's hand was devoid of a ring. It was a passing thought that didn't surface again until J.J. and Zoey took their leave and walked on toward the house.

"I heard you ask Dr. Blair about her son," J.J. said, not trying to mask her curiosity.

"Nickolas—he's four, and the cutest kid." Zoey turned her face up to J.J. "He was really sick a couple of years ago. My dad said he had blood cancer. Delaney quit being a vet for a while. Everybody was afraid Nick might die. But he got better. I'm glad. I love him and his mom."

"Is his father a local rancher?"

Zoey shook her head. "Delaney's not married. Nickolas is like me, he's only got one parent. 'Cept my mom died, and his dad left before Nick was born. He doesn't live in this country," Zoey said, climbing the steps to the back porch.

An almost foreign emotion rippled through J.J. for reasons she was loath to admit. Jealousy. Delaney Blair was gorgeous, capable and unmarried. Add to that, Zoey loved the woman and her son. Earlier, Mack had spoken approvingly of the vet.

"Will you take my picture after we clean the eggs, J.J.?"

J.J. sent the green-eyed monster away. Jealousy wasn't an admirable trait. She had no call to resent a seemingly nice woman. And she had absolutely no right to the slightest proprietary twinge when it came to Mack Bannerman. "Let me see about Erma. I'll come back and we'll clean the eggs, then I'll get my cameras and we'll have some fun."

"Somebody on TV said a good photographer can airbrush away flaws and wrinkles. Can you get rid of my freckles?" Zoey brushed at one cheek. "I hate them."

J.J. tilted her head. "They're you, Zoey. A good photographer brings out the natural beauty of a subject. Promise me you'll reserve judgment about keeping your freckles until after I print copies? By the way, where's your dad's printer?"

"In his office. It takes a password. He'll probably give it to you, but I don't have it." She screwed up her nose. "I told you he and Erma still think I'm a kid."

J.J. laughed. "You *are* a kid. I'm sure they see that you're precocious for your age."

"Is that another word I need to look up in the dictionary?" Zoey sighed. J.J. laughed again and went to check on Erma.

Chapter Six

"Erma's still asleep," J.J. said, rejoining Zoey in the kitchen. "Let's finish dealing with these eggs. While we work, give me some ideas about where you'd like to have your picture taken."

"At school they use this background sheet that's blue with white clouds. We line up alphabetically by grade. They call your name, you stand in front of the clouds and the camera guy says, 'Smile.' The other kids in line make dorky faces. I try not to laugh, but I still look weird."

J.J. laughed. "I hear you. My elementary and junior high photos were ridiculously bad. I wore braces for four years and didn't want them to show, so my mouth always looked funny." J.J. cleaned a few eggs. "I'd like to try several settings. How do you feel about us fixing your hair in some new styles?"

"Okay, I guess. I've worn braids forever. I tried a ponytail but everybody said my ears stuck out." Zoey broke an egg in her annoyance. "Oh, yikes. Sorry." She scooped the slippery yolk out of the sink and dumped it in the trash.

"I'm sure everybody doesn't think that," J.J. said matter-of-factly.

The pair worked in silence until all the eggs were cleaned. "My camera equipment is in my room," J.J. said. "Follow me. I'll see what accessories I brought that we can use to shake up your look."

"You mean like hair clips or scrunchies?"

"More like hats, belts, scarves and jackets." She laughed. "I always travel with stuff."

"Cool." Zoey's excitement was reflected by the spring in her step.

The first thing J.J. did was unbraid Zoey's hair. "You have thick, lovely hair," she said, finger-combing the loose strands.

"I wish it was a different color. It's not red. It's not even brown. And it's so straight I can't do anything but braid it."

"Have you tried using a curling iron?"

"No."

"Give me a minute to plug mine in. I love an iron for instant curl. You have a nice natural wave." J.J. studied Zoey's rust-red hair with a critical eye. The blunt cut ends reached the middle of the girl's back. "There are shampoos that will bring out your red highlights."

"Really? Erma buys whatever shampoo is on sale at our general store."

"Hmm." J.J. made a mental note to send Zoey samples from her salon. "While the iron heats up, try on my gray jacket. It may look a little big, but I can adjust it." J.J. removed it from the hanger. She opened the top dresser drawer and brought out a black felt hat and a bright teal scarf.

"This jacket is so cool. And it fits pretty good," Zoey exclaimed.

"I like it because it goes with a lot of things. If you buy classic pieces they'll last, too." She tested the curling iron and beckoned Zoey to sit on the end of the bed. Working quickly, J.J. soon had Zoey in curls.

Sorting through her makeup bag, J.J. chose a container of eye shadow. "I'll apply the faintest tint of green to your eyelids, so close your eyes."

She made a light sweep over Zoey's lids. "Now a colorless gloss to make your lips shine," she said. When she finished, Zoey turned toward the mirror.

"Don't look until I comb out your hair." Blocking Zoey's view, J.J. brushed out the curl, and after rubbing her hands with a splotch of mousse she fluffed Zoey's hair. Deftly looping a bright scarf around her neck, J.J. stepped back. "Now look. We're ready to take photographs."

For a long moment Zoey could only stare at herself. "Awesome possum," she finally said. "I...look... different. Way better. If the pictures turn out good, will you print a big one so I can frame it to give my dad for his birthday?"

"Sure! It shouldn't be a problem if we get a pose you like. That's right, your dad's birthday is next month. June 1st, isn't it?"

"Wow!" Zoey's eyes bugged. "You remember my dad's birthday?"

J.J. felt a flush rise. "We, uh, had a group of friends at college who celebrated everyone's birthdays. It was a long time ago, though. Come on outside." J.J. picked up the felt hat and her camera bag.

Zoey took a last look in the mirror and moved a curl caught on the scarf.

"I love outdoor shots," J.J. said. "I'll pose you by

a tree, by the corral and standing beside a horse. Do you have one of your own? A horse?"

"There are two I used to ride a lot. Misty is about the color of this jacket." Zoey ran a hand down the wool. "Splash is a pinto. I'm sure my dad left them here, because the wranglers have their own cutting horses."

J.J. posed Zoey near a fence post with her booted foot on the lowest rail. She backed up and took a camera out of her bag. "Look toward the barn. Tilt your chin down a bit. Great. Imagine you're eating your favorite ice cream." J.J. clicked off several shots. "Now picture something you want, but can't have. Excellent. Turn your face toward me. Fantastic!" *Click, click, click.* J.J. dropped to one knee and took a few photos from that angle, too. "Okay, on to the horses."

In the barn she consulted her light meter, then set up an LED light bar. "Do you think this will be too bright for the pinto? I think his coat offers the best contrast of colors."

Shaking her head, Zoey walked to a row of stalls where both the pinto and the gray gazed solemnly over gates. "Splash is really gentle. Should I saddle him?"

"No, I want close-ups of your heads together."

Zoey clipped a lead rope around the pinto's neck and led him out of the stall. All the while, J.J. bobbed and dipped, taking frame after frame. Pausing briefly, she walked over, patted the horse, then arranged the hat atop Zoey's curls.

"Hey, Splash is trying to eat your hat." Ducking, Zoey laughed and pushed the pinto's nose away.

"Priceless," J.J. murmured, clicking away. "Your dad will love one of those. Or I can create a collage.

Okay, put Splash back in his stall. I need to check on Erma, and I'm going to grab my gold suit jacket for you to wear next. And I have a new idea for your hair."

"I like my hair like this." Zoey led the horse away. J.J. was packing up her equipment when the girl returned.

"I'm pretty sure you'll like what I have in mind. This time I'll add pink to your lips."

"Sometime this summer Brandy's mom is taking her to get her ears pierced. They're going to a big department store where someone will show Brandy how to use makeup."

J.J. detected envy in Zoey's words. "Can you ask your dad to see if Brandy's mom will take you, too? She's your best friend, after all."

"Brandy invited me…"

There was a *but* at the end of that sentence. Perhaps she ought to mind her own business, J.J. thought. Mack had hesitated when she'd asked if she could photograph Zoey. He might hate these photos—maybe he didn't want to see Zoey in any makeup at all. Rural ranchers weren't necessarily progressive.

Arriving at the patio, J.J. set her camera bag on the outdoor table. "Go on into my room. If Erma's awake, we can bring her out for some fresh air."

"Can we take more pictures later?"

"Sure, or I can take another batch tomorrow. It's getting hot, and sun rays bounce off all kinds of things and ruin photographs."

Zoey loped across the flagstones and flung her arms around J.J. "This has been the best day ever. I wish you lived in La Mesa."

J.J. froze, startled by the realization that she wished

she lived in La Mesa, too. She managed to hug Zoey back. "What would you be doing with your day if Erma was well and I wasn't here?" she asked lightly.

Zoey shrugged. "I'd read, or go help Brandy pick vegetables. If Brandy came over, Erma would sit out here and knit while we went for a swim. We do that a lot during the summer. And we only have one more half day of school."

"Hmm, well, it'll be lunchtime soon. It's up to us to prepare something. What should we have?"

"Soup and grilled cheese sandwiches," Zoey said, not missing a beat.

"That sounds easy. I hope Erma's awake."

But she wasn't when J.J. slipped into her room. So J.J. called, "Erma, if you get up we'll eat lunch. Then you can phone the doctor about your medicine."

Erma opened one eye a slit. "Jill? I'm so tired. Is there something you need, dear?"

"You've been asleep since Mack left. I've been out taking pictures of Zoey, but it's nearly lunchtime."

"That long? Mercy." Erma pressed a hand to her head. "It's noon, you say?"

"Not quite. More like eleven-fifteen."

"Can you let me sleep till twelve? Doctors at the clinic probably go out for lunch."

"All right, I'll come back in forty-five minutes. Is your hip causing you pain?"

"Once I take two of those pills I don't feel anything. With that medicine a body can sleep like Rip van Winkle."

J.J. smiled, glad at least that Erma could still crack a joke. "I hope it's a healing sleep."

Erma's eyes were already closing, and J.J. detected

a slowing of her breath. Sighing, she decided to go shoot the rest of Zoey's photos.

Zoey sat in J.J.'s bedroom. "Is Erma awake?"

"Not really. I promised to let her sleep a while longer. So let's redo your hair and try the gold jacket. I'll take a few pictures in the living room and some on the patio with the pool as a backdrop. Then I'll wake Erma and we'll make lunch. How does that sound?"

"Okay. Is Erma all right? This isn't like her. She's always up before me every morning, and she's busy even after I go to bed. She *will* wake up, won't she? I mean...she's not dying?"

Seeing how worried Zoey was, J.J. sat beside her on the bed. "I don't have any medical training, but I truly believe it's the pills knocking her for a loop. I promise you, Zoey, if I saw the slightest sign it was more, I'd pack her off to the clinic ASAP. All right?" In a reflexive action, J.J. brushed away the curls falling into Zoey's eyes.

Zoey smiled weakly. "I trust you, J.J."

Those few simple words flustered J.J., but at the same time made her heart swell. Trust had been totally broken between her and Zoey's dad. And now his child, the product of the relationship that had caused that long-ago breakup, trusted *her*. This humbled her and made her throat tighten, so when she jumped up and said, "Since that's settled, let's get you ready for the next round of photos," it came out sounding like a croak.

Had things gone differently for her and Mack, J.J. might well be preparing their *daughter for photographs.* Swallowing, she took a shaky breath and grabbed a hairbrush. "What I have in mind is called a crown of braids. It's a favorite style with young Hollywood stars and models." Going behind Zoey, J.J. separated her hair into chunks and made loose French braids that feathered around the girl's forehead. The braids met in the center back of her head. J.J. wove them together with the rest of Zoey's hair, creating a sophisticated look.

"Oh, I love it," Zoey said, peering at herself in the mirror. "It's still braids, but looks more girlie than what I usually wear. Will you teach me how to do this?"

"It's easier to have someone else do it. But I can teach Erma."

The gold suit jacket was a little big on Zoey. J.J. rolled up the sleeves so the satin lining showed, and belted it in at the waist with a narrow gold chain.

They went back to the patio, and J.J. posed Zoey beside greenery flanking one end of the pool. In the middle of a round of shots, J.J. was startled when she zoomed in for a close-up of Zoey. She had a sudden sense of déjà vu that made her pull back from her Nikon. It felt as if she'd taken the same shot, but a long time ago. It was something about Zoey's wide hazel eyes, and the way the sun reddened her hair. Her cheeks, with their smattering of golden freckles, looked very familiar.

Zoey stiffened. "J.J., is something wrong?"

"No, no." It was probably nothing. Warmth brushed her back and she began to relax. After all, she took scores of photos of young models.

"We should go inside to shoot, though," J.J. said. "And get a drink of water. It's really hot."

Zoey sprang up from the chaise longue. "My dad

says people who aren't used to our Texas sun should drink lots of water."

"I've been away from Texas a long time," J.J. murmured. That weird sensation was probably brought on by dehydration.

After guzzling some water, J.J. took a dozen more pictures inside.

"Let's call it a wrap," she said, capping her lens. "If I haven't gotten more good photos than you can choose from, I've lost my touch." She grinned cheekily.

"I hope you did. Every one of my school photos has been horrible. And the snapshots Erma and my dad take on holidays…they're awful, too."

"Do other people like them?" J.J. asked as they returned to J.J.'s room. "Often we're too critical of ourselves."

"My dad buys the school packet, anyway. He started an album when I was a baby and he *always* does a new page every school year. We give a picture to Grandmother and Granddad Adams. Granddad always says my mom was way prettier."

"What? He should be ashamed!" J.J. snapped before she could remind herself that it wasn't her place to criticize Zoey's grandparents.

"My dad argues with him. But they don't exactly get along." Zoey unfastened the belt and handed it back to J.J. She slipped off the jacket and hung it on a hanger, frowning. "He's never said anything to me, but Erma told me that after my mom died, Granddad Adams thought they should raise me. Daddy said no. They hired a lawyer and so did he. Daddy's lawyer won. Erma says my grandparents don't act like the Christians they're supposed to be."

Thinking Zoey carried quite a weight for a kid, J.J. stored her camera and offered an understanding smile. "Tell you what, if you get out the stuff for lunch, I'll wake Erma up. Maybe later we can go to town for ice cream, if Erma's up to the drive."

"Can I keep these braids?"

"Sure. I'm glad you like your hair. I think it's a great look for you, Zoey."

"And can I call Brandy to see if she wants to take a break and come with us? I want her to see my hair."

"Inviting Brandy is fine by me, but we need to play it by ear. It all depends on how Erma feels."

"I know. J.J., I wish Benny's cousin couldn't ever come and that you'd stay forever."

"Don't cross off Benny's poor cousin until you've met her," J.J. rushed to say, afraid of what else Zoey might wish. "I'm sure she'll be a better cook than I am."

"But you know a bunch of other stuff. You'd be the best mother. Hey, you're my dad's age. Why didn't you ever get married and have kids, J.J.?"

A knot formed in J.J.'s stomach. She took a minute to cobble together a story appropriate for the child of the only man she'd ever wanted to marry. "Zoey, some careers demand as much time and energy as a marriage. It's not fair to short-change a boss, or a husband and kids."

"Oh." Zoey's face fell.

"Don't look so glum. Not all careers require time away from family. You have a lot of careers to choose from, and years to pick one. I'll go get Erma if you set out what we need for grilled cheese sandwiches."

"Gosh, we didn't wash the breakfast dishes."

"I told your dad I'd only run the dishwasher after supper, to conserve water. You probably know all about the drought?"

"Brother, do I. Dad thinks I should take a three-minute shower instead of a bath." Zoey made a face. "I like to read in the bathtub. You can't read in the shower."

J.J. laughed. "You're a girl after my own heart. I also light votive candles and settle in my tub with a book and a glass of wine. See, that shows I'm too self-indulgent to do right by a husband and kids."

"No, you're not." Zoey shook her head.

J.J. went to Erma's room, feeling hollow. The sad truth was that the more time she spent with Zoey, the more J.J. regretted not being a mother.

"Erma? Good. You're awake. Zoey wants soup and grilled cheese sandwiches for lunch."

"That girl would eat grilled cheese seven days a week." Erma covered a yawn even as she levered herself into a sitting position. "Ow, ow, ow!" She grabbed her hip. "I'm okay lying down. The minute I bend my hip to sit, it feels like someone stabbed me. Not that I really know what it feels like to be stabbed," she muttered.

"You're probably tired of me saying that healing takes time." J.J. steadied the wheelchair. "It's all I can say. That and I'm sorry you're in pain."

Erma eased out of bed into the chair. "The doctor did tell me I'd be laid up four to six weeks. I didn't want to believe he was right. It looks like he might know what he's talking about, so I should get better at working this contraption. Wait here, Jill. If I can't manage on my own in the bathroom, I'll holler."

"I don't mind lending a hand."

"I've been taking care of myself for over fifty years and taking care of this family more than half of that. Needing help goes against the grain."

J.J. understood, so she straightened the bed while she waited. Erma managed, and even combed her hair.

"Why don't you phone the clinic and ask about your medicine while I get the soup going?" J.J. said as they entered the kitchen. She handed Erma her cell phone and the pill bottle.

"I need the phone number off that yellow invoice," Erma said, pointing to the counter.

Zoey retrieved the paper and gave Erma a hug.

J.J. half listened to Erma's side of the conversation while she sliced cheese. "Then it's okay to take one pill during the day and two at bedtime?" Erma asked. From the way her head went up and down like a bobblehead doll, J.J. could tell those were the revised directions.

"I like what you did with your hair," Erma said to Zoey once she was off the phone.

"J.J. fixed it two new ways. She used a curling iron first. Do you think I can buy one?"

"You can ask your dad."

They sat down to lunch. "I feel better already knowing I can cut back on my pills," Erma said. "I wouldn't have questioned the doctor. Thanks for nudging me, Jill."

"Do you want to be called Jill or J.J.?" Zoey asked.

"Either. I answer to 'Hey, photographer' a lot, too," she said, laughing.

Erma gestured with half her sandwich. "Jill is such a pretty name. Why use initials? They sound harsh."

"Initials sound more professional. When I started out in this business, a helpful magazine editor told me a name can make the difference in being selected or not."

"Seems weird," Zoey said. "Erma, if you feel better, can J.J. drive us to town for ice cream?"

"I don't feel that peppy. You girls go ahead without me."

J.J. was proud of Zoey, who was the first to say, "No, we can't go off and leave you alone."

So they all stayed home and spent a pleasant afternoon by the pool.

Later, after a light salad supper, Erma said, "If I wait to take my night pills, I'll be awake longer. Is anyone up for a game of dominos?"

"If you teach me," J.J. said. "I've never played."

Zoey ran to get the box and J.J. cleared the table. She soon discovered they were both cutthroat players. "I can't think as fast as you add up the spots," she said halfway through the game. "Zoey, you must be a whiz at math."

Erma reached over and patted Zoey's arm. "She's a whiz at everything. This girl gets straight *A*s. Her dad is so proud of her. Me, too."

Zoey blushed and ducked her head. Erma turned to J.J. "I said it before, but I'll say it again…it's nice having you around. You're what Zoey needs." Erma then muttered half under her breath, "And Mackenzie, too."

J.J. bypassed that comment. "Are we going to finish this game? If not, I'm ready to call it a night. I can barely keep my eyes open."

Erma won the round, and Zoey put the game away before going upstairs to bed. J.J. got Erma water to take her pills and settled her for the night. Then she loaded the washing machine, hoping that running it at the same time as the dishwasher wasn't using too much water. She sat on the patio until it was time to switch loads, then went out again with a glass of wine while the first load dried. It wasn't until after she'd folded the towels and crossed the patio in the moonlight that she thought about meeting Mack out there. And wow, his kiss. *Was she what he and Zoey needed?* Recalling his reaction, sadness overtook her.

THE CATTLE WERE always restless following a move. Mack, Benny and the wranglers took turns in pairs riding through the herd during the night. Eldon played a harmonica, and the animals seemed to stop milling to listen. The sound soothed Mack, too. He'd always loved spending hours out with the cattle.

As the sun rose on a new day, Benny and Mack met on a knoll overlooking the green valley, now awash with red-coated cows. "What do you think, Benny?"

"They'll calm down once they discover there's water in the river."

Mack leaned on his saddle horn. "They seem extra edgy to me. I'm going to leave Eldon and Trevor out here for another day. I need to get back to the ranch."

"You're the one on edge, Mackenzie."

"Having Jill back messes with my head."

"Your head, huh?"

"She's just passing through, Benny."

"Maybe she'd stay if some stubborn old mule would ask her."

Mack loosened his reins. "I'm going down to make coffee. Then we need to round up strays and do a count. I want to be back to Turkey Creek by noon."

THE NEXT MORNING, Erma got up to try J.J.'s attempt at French toast. Oddly, J.J. missed bantering with the men at breakfast.

Zoey said, "I got up early. Daddy said if I feed the horses and chickens and gather eggs without complaining, he'll think about getting me a cell phone when school starts."

"Young lady, you should help with chores without having to be bribed," Erma said.

Zoey grimaced as she brought her plate to the counter.

J.J. stacked the dirty dishes. "Zoey, the vet said we should turn the cow and her calf out to pasture after feeding her this morning. Do you want to do that now?"

"I don't know which pasture since all the other cows are up at the summer range. Dad and Benny should be home this afternoon. Will it hurt to leave the cow and her calf in the barn and let my dad put them where he wants them?"

"I guess not." J.J. rinsed their breakfast dishes while Zoey emptied the dishwasher. "Should we wait until the men show up before we eat lunch?"

Erma, who still seemed groggy, shrugged. "You can do up a Jell-O salad now, and serve it with tuna sandwiches. That'll keep if for some reason they don't get back until later."

"Okay," J.J. said. "I saw packs of gelatin in the pantry. Anyone have a request for what kind?"

"Orange with mandarin oranges. Erma fixes it like that," Zoey said. "This is the bowl she uses. Do you make up three packs and two cans of oranges?" she asked, leaning on the arm of Erma's wheelchair.

"If all the men come in I'd double that."

"You must cook boatloads of food," J.J. said. "Do you ever run out of ideas?"

"It's routine," Erma said. "I like to cook more than cleaning house or doing mountains of dirty laundry. Speaking of laundry, did I dream I heard the washer and dryer running last night?"

"I ran a load of jeans and also towels. I folded everything and left stacks on the dryer. I'll put another load in now. Shirts," she said, pausing to see if anyone objected. No one did.

"I believe I'll have one of you wheel me out to the patio while you do morning chores," Erma said. "I'm so used to running in and out that yesterday I felt cooped up."

"I'll set you up out there with a pitcher of iced tea if Zoey grabs the egg baskets. There, does this look right?" J.J. asked.

Zoey peered into the Jell-O bowl. "Looks yummy. I love the smell of oranges, don't you, J.J.?"

"Orange is nice. I like vanilla, too. And cinnamon. There may be an orange scent to the shampoo I told you about. I'll send you some to try."

"You'd send me stuff all the way from New York?" Zoey watched J.J. make room in the refrigerator for the bowl.

"It's no big deal. Working with models like I do, I see the latest, greatest products. My salon can order almost anything on the market."

"I can't imagine having so many choices," Erma said, gazing at Zoey. "We're lucky the general store stocks tried-and-true products that don't cost a mint."

Zoey rolled her eyes, prompting J.J. to recall the girl's earlier remark about shampoo from the general store. "I like my hair to smell good," she said. "Specialty products offer more variety."

"Huh," Erma responded. "I'll grab the pitcher of tea while you load the washer. Then we can go outside. It's gonna be a scorcher. There's a breeze, but a hot one. We may only stay by the pool a little while."

For early spring, the heat felt oppressive. J.J. parked Erma in the shade and said to Zoey, "If you want to feed the livestock, I'll go straight to the chicken coop. Erma's right about it being stifling. Let's divide up the chores so we'll finish faster and be back in the shade sooner."

"Suits me. Don't worry if there aren't as many eggs today, J.J. When it gets superhot the hens don't lay as many."

"I don't blame them." J.J. laughed. "The roosters get to strut around catching a breeze while the hens have to sit on those warm nests."

That comment made Zoey giggle.

They met again within half an hour outside the barn. "Hey, we're both done," Zoey exclaimed, blotting her sweating forehead on her arm. "Race you to the patio. I hope there's still ice in that pitcher of tea."

"You go on. I don't want to risk breaking any eggs. You were right—I only got one full basket instead of two."

Zoey slowed her steps. "I can wait and walk with you."

"No, no. Go ahead. Pour me a glass of tea." Zoey, who didn't need a second urging, took off at a dead run. J.J. shook her head, wishing she had as much energy. As she neared the patio, she noticed puffs of dust rising in the distance. She watched as the line moved toward the ranch. Setting her basket of eggs on the table, she nudged Erma. "Look to the west. Do you think someone is moving a herd? Or could it be a dust storm building? We had those when I lived in Lubbock. This land is so flat and dry I imagine they'd be fiercer here."

Erma shaded her eyes. "Mercy." She gripped J.J.'s forearm. "That's not dust, its smoke. A grass fire. Headed our way. I don't mean to alarm you, but three weeks ago, a rancher south of town lost his barn in a grass fire."

"I *am* alarmed," J.J. said, digging her cell phone out of her pocket. "Should I call the local fire department? Surely someone needs to know."

"Call 9-1-1 and report its location relative to Turkey Creek Ranch. They put out an alarm and all the available ranchers gather out there with water barrels and wet gunnysacks. They form a chain and beat back the flames. We'd better make tracks outta here, Jill. Dang, what a time for our menfolk to be away."

J.J. held up a hand to quiet Erma, and reported the fire as concisely as she could to the dispatcher on the phone. "They'll sound an alarm and get firefighters and ranchers right on it," she said, pocketing her phone. "Erma, we can't leave without wetting down some of this area in case fire reaches the ranch before they can put it out."

"What can we do?" Erma asked. "A woman, a girl and a hurt old lady."

Zoey started to cry. She scooted her chair around and tucked her head against Erma's shoulder. "I don't want our house to burn down."

"Listen," J.J. said. "Let's collect some important things from the house while we have time. Mack's pickup is here. Erma, do you know where he keeps his keys? We can load up the bed. I'll park it on the main road, and I can connect those hoses I saw in the barn, too. You and Zoey wet the barn and house siding while I take the horses, the cow and the calf to the creek."

"Mack leaves his keys in his truck," Erma said. "The ranch records are on the laptop computer on his office desk. Zoey, you know where the suitcases are in the hall closet. Jill's right, we each need to pack a bag with essentials. Now get going." She passed Zoey the egg basket.

The girl hesitated until J.J. said she'd meet her in the kitchen. Casting a last glance at the gray puffs she now knew were smoke, J.J. wheeled Erma toward the house. "We have some time," she told the others. "The fire line is still quite a ways out from the ranch."

Chapter Seven

"I'm scared," Zoey said, hauling two suitcases into Erma's room. "If our house burns down, where will we live?"

J.J. took one suitcase, opened it and set it on Erma's bed. She opened the lower dresser drawers to make it easier for Erma to get her belongings. "We'll do everything we can to keep that from happening, Zoey."

"I want Daddy."

She wasn't alone on that score. "I know, honey. We can try to call him after we collect everything and move his pickup to safety. Your dad said some of the summer pasture is out of cellular range. Although, if he and Benny are headed home, he may be closer to a cell tower. You can try calling him from the house phone after we get the pickup packed up. Regardless, Zoey, he can't help until he gets back, so we need to prepare. Okay?"

Zoey nodded, but still seemed frozen to the spot.

J.J. handed the second suitcase to the girl. "The wildfire is still a ways off. Hurry…go pack some undies, pajamas, jeans, shirts…whatever fits in this bag. Bring it out to your dad's pickup and I'll meet you there. Erma, I'll come back after I see to the animals."

J.J. gave Zoey a big hug before dashing out across the patio. She didn't want to look at the creeping fire, but couldn't help herself. If anything, the band stretched wider but still seemed like dust.

She ran to the barn. The two horses obviously sensed that something was amiss. They whickered and shifted restlessly in their stalls. Yesterday she had seen Zoey take lead ropes from a wall hook. Locating them, she grabbed two and looped one around the neck of each horse before leading the horses outside. The pinto snorted and his nostrils flared. J.J. wasn't sure how far it was down to Turkey Creek. She'd gone there a couple of times in the past to make out with Mack. That was long ago, but thankfully landscapes didn't change.

Only people did.

The stream was closer than she remembered. She considered wading across it to tie the animals to saplings on the other side. She was worried that if the fire reached this point and sparks jumped the creek, the horses might still be lost. Trusting that Mack could track them if they bolted, she freed the pair slapped their rumps so they'd cross the stream, and raced back to the barn. The cow and her calf were harder to budge. J.J. tugged and pulled and even cursed the heifer. Finally, she scooped up the gangling calf and jogged down to the stream, hoping the mother would follow. *She did.* Relieved, J.J. left them both at the water's edge.

Panic rose when she thought about everything that might be lost. Mack's family history was here. That spurred her to hurry and unlatch the chicken coop. She propped it open with a rock. If the fire didn't reach the ranch, Mack might hate her for releasing all his livestock. *So be it.*

Zoey was standing nervously next to the pickup. J.J. hauled two hoses out of the barn and asked, "Do you know where we can connect these?"

"There's a faucet next to the front porch at the house, and… Oh, there's another…a tall pipe out by the corral. I tried calling Daddy, but he didn't answer. Where's Erma?"

"I haven't been back to the house. Would you go see if she's ready and help wheel her out? I'll connect these. Then if you and Erma begin soaking the buildings and the grass by the barn, I'll grab more stuff from the house. Things like the family pictures hanging in the hall, and the laptop—"

"I didn't pack my photo album," Zoey broke in. "Or the picture of my mom. It's on my nightstand." Tears spilled over her freckles.

"Sweetie, run and get them now. And any important mementos you can carry. Listen. Sirens. If they make a fire break between us and the fire, we'll probably do all of this preparation for nothing."

"I hope so." Zoey ran back to the house and J.J. uncoiled both hoses. She stretched them out full length and tightened their connectors to the faucets, giving each an extra wrench. Her head spun because there was so much to do.

Erma had wheeled herself to the patio and had managed, however awkwardly, to drag her suitcase along.

"Let me carry that. Erma, why didn't you wait for me or Zoey? You'll hurt your hip again. Here, take this hose. I'll turn on the water and you spray as much of this side of the house and the surrounding ground as you can."

Picking up the suitcase, J.J. detoured by the front of the house. After turning on the faucet, she set the suitcase in the pickup bed next to Zoey's bag.

"Erma, I'm going in to rescue Mack's family pictures. You mentioned his laptop. Can you think of anything else I need to grab for him?"

"He has a checkbook and ledger in his middle desk drawer. His clothes would be in his bedroom. If you can, grab a few things out of his closet. It's good of you to think about his family photographs."

J.J. took off for the house again at a run. In no time she returned, her arms piled high with photo albums and frames, and Mack's jeans and shirts flapping from hangers. Over her shoulder was draped an old crocheted bedspread she'd spotted on a quilt rack in Mack's bedroom. He had a couple of photographs on his wall, but she'd been too weighed down to grab them.

"I'd forgotten all about the bedspread," Erma shouted over to J.J. "Mack will appreciate you saving it. It's one of few things he has left that belonged to his mother."

Zoey staggered out of the house, bowed under the weight of her treasures. J.J. noticed a couple of stuffed animals, red boots, some books and a photo album. Helping the girl put her load into the pickup, J.J. caught sight of an eight-by-ten framed photo of Faith Adams—well, Faith Bannerman. But the photo was premarriage. Faith wore a cap and gown. Judging by how young she looked, J.J. guessed it was her high school graduation picture. Taking care to cushion the glass frame between Zoey's stuffed toys, J.J. wondered how she'd missed finding Mack and Faith's wedding pictures. There hadn't been any among the family portraits in the hall or the wedding photo albums.

"Zoey, I need you to turn on the water to the hose I connected by the corral. Wet the ground between the corral and barn. That entire area is dry grass. I'll go move your dad's pickup to the highway. Back soon."

"Did you try calling my dad? Shouldn't *we* leave now, too?"

"I'm pretty sure he and Benny are headed home by now. I think he'd want us to do everything possible to save the ranch before we go."

"But he'd ride faster if he knew we're in trouble."

"I'll phone as soon as I move his pickup. Come to think of it…I don't have his cell number."

Zoey rattled it off, and J.J. hoped she got it right over the roar of the pickup motor. She crossed the highway and parked in a pull-out on the opposite side. The fire would have to jump two lanes of asphalt to reach Mack's pickup, she thought as she pocketed his keys. Returning at a run, she called the number Zoey had given her. Mack's phone rang twice, then cut off. She tried a second time but it went straight to voice mail. When she attempted to leave a message all she got was static.

By now she felt grimy. Somehow she'd scratched the underside of one arm and also had a bloody gash on her right knee. She waved at Zoey and Erma, then darted into her room. J.J. contemplated whether it'd be smart to trade the shorts she wore for jeans. But that would mean tugging off her boots—precious time better spent helping wet the house and barn. She haphazardly tossed a few clothes in her bag and carried it and her camera bag outside. Turning her rented SUV around, she gauged how far away to leave it so she could still wheel Erma over the bumpy terrain, load everyone and scoot out to the highway if it seemed they'd lose the battle to the encroaching blaze.

For the first time she smelled smoke. Her stomach tensed. The gray line had moved closer and billowed higher. Now she could actually see red-orange flames licking along the ground amid the acrid odor driven toward them on the hot breeze.

"Erma, how are you holding up?" J.J. yelled, choking a little on the taste of smoke.

"I'm okay," Erma said into the crook of her arm. "Look over there! La Mesa's fire trucks are pumping water, and our neighbors are trying to beat out the flames with soaked gunnysacks, just like I told you. There's nothing there but dry grass, but I can't tell if they're making headway."

"Me, either. We'll do what we can, but we need to give ourselves time to make tracks out of here no matter what."

"You won't get an argument out of me. Right now I think the barn is in the most worrisome spot. I wish this danged hose was longer. I have more water pressure than Zoey does coming out of that well."

"I didn't see any other hoses in the barn. But I brought buckets. I'll go fill them at the creek. If I saturate the ground around the small corral, maybe the rails won't catch fire. We'll have to hope that and Zoey's efforts will stop the flames short of the barn."

"Jilly, dear, don't be killing yourself hauling water.

It's not far down to the creek, but it's all uphill coming back."

J.J. heard the slight wheeze in Erma's voice and feared the smoke was getting to the older woman. She debated loading everyone up right now. But the line of fire moving steadily toward Mack's barn seemed to be getting ahead of the people fighting it.

Dashing back to the kitchen, J.J. wet three dish towels and hurried outside again. She tied one around Erma's nose and mouth and the second around Zoey's face, taking the third for herself.

"Did you get Daddy on his cell?"

J.J. shook her head. "I tried twice, kiddo." She hated to see how Zoey's shoulders slumped.

It dawned on her that the pool was much closer than Turkey Creek, so she took her buckets there. In spite of how the flagstone hurt her knees when she dropped down, she filled both buckets and ran as quickly as she could to the corral. She dumped the water on the yellowed grass around the posts most in danger from the approaching fire. She repeated the process several times until her back and arms ached and her legs shook, threatening to give out.

The last time she passed Zoey, who was still valiantly spraying water on the lower part of the barn and the ground between it and the corral, the girl slipped the towel off her mouth. "J.J., I'm hot and tired. Can we please get out of here?"

Skidding to a stop, J.J. took note of Zoey's red-rimmed eyes and figured her own must look as bad. A fire truck lumbered through the pasture that led to the creek, and J.J. heard the empty pumper sucking up creek water.

Nodding, unable to speak through the thickening smoke mixed with tears that clogged her throat, she set down her buckets and propped Zoey's still-running hose through one handle so it would continue to spray the barn planks after they left. Looping an arm around Zoey's shoulders, they hastened to Erma.

"We have to go," J.J. said. She turned off Erma's hose because the people fighting the blaze had pretty much stamped out the fire headed for the house. The corral and barn still sat in its path. J.J. was afraid that if the barn caught, flying embers could ignite the house. She banished her fear. "We gave it our best shot," she said, her voice little more than a rasp as she took the handles of Erma's wheelchair with smoke-blackened hands, and the three of them hustled to the SUV.

Zoey climbed into the backseat and buckled in. She buried her face in the wet towel while J.J. boosted Erma into the passenger seat, collapsed the wheelchair and tossed it into the back. She slid behind the steering wheel, noticing how filthy her bare legs were, but just before she closed the door, she heard a dog barking.

"It's Jiggs!" Zoey dropped her towel and released the catch on her seat belt. "Daddy's home! Daddy's home," she shouted, flinging open the back door.

"Wait," J.J. implored, but it was too late. Zoey had already burst out of the truck, falling to her knees in the gravel parking strip to greet the collie.

Mack and Benny must have galloped their horses around the pool and across the patio. They bore down on the SUV. Mack was first to dismount, and was nearly bowled over by Zoey, who'd scrambled up and launched herself at him with arms widespread.

"You're covered in soot. What the hell?" He met
J.J.'s eyes with fury as he lifted Zoey back into the
SUV. "I gave you credit for having good sense, Jill. I
need to help fight this fire. Do you suppose you could
manage to get my family out of imminent danger? Oh,
and take Jiggs and our horses." He snapped his fingers
until the dog bounded in next to Zoey. Gathering the
reins of his and Benny's lathered horses, Mack tied
them to J.J.'s back bumper. "And where's my pickup?"

J.J. stabbed a finger toward the main road where
the rear of his pickup was barely visible. Her throat
was so parched she had no voice left to defend herself. He slammed both open doors of her SUV and
she jumped. Mack clearly expected her to follow his
imperious order, because he turned away and ran to
help Benny unroll a long, fat blue hose from the pool's
pump to the corral. Within seconds J.J. saw water
gush out of the hose to flood the whole interior of the
small corral. She put the SUV into gear and realized
how much her palms hurt from being rubbed nearly
raw by the bucket handles—she'd lost track of how
many heavy buckets of water she'd carried from the
pool to the corral.

"They're using the pool's back-flush system," she
whispered to Erma. "Why didn't I think of that?" She
underwent a coughing fit that slowed their departure.

Erma patted her back. "Mack doesn't know what
you've done, Jill. Put yourself in his shoes. Grass fires
burned out two ranches earlier this spring. I'm sure
he and Benny saw the fire from a ways out. They'd
know the ranch is in its path. Fear drove them to ride
hard. Look how sweaty those horses are."

"Yeah," Zoey said from the backseat. "Daddy

sometimes yells at me if he's afraid I'd get hurt doing something. He always says he's sorry and he doesn't stay mad, because he loves me."

J.J. drove to the main highway and parked. She was shaking too hard to go farther, and she didn't want to drag the plodding horses.

"Are you all right?" Erma asked in a low voice.

J.J. scrubbed a trembling hand over her face. "Belated reaction to a crisis. Or possibly from Jiggs's cold nose in my ear," she said, trying to make light of her wooziness as she reached back to nudge the dog away.

"Jiggs wants to go with my dad," Zoey said, trying to tug the animal onto her lap. "He's supposed to be my dog, but he likes being with my dad best."

"That's because he was born to herd," Erma said. "Your father is generally out with the cattle."

"Dad says it's because I never get up in time to feed Jiggs, and the person who feeds a dog becomes his best friend."

Dry as her throat was, J.J. had to laugh—if not at the truth of Zoey's claim, at the strange normalcy of this conversation when they weren't so far removed from danger.

"Listen," Zoey exclaimed, unbuckling her seat belt to slide over to J.J.'s side of the vehicle. "Maybe they almost have the fire out. There's only trails of smoke out past the barn. Out where the fire trucks are. The people who came in pickups and helped are talking to Benny and my dad. There's Brandy's dad. He must've left work to help. Brandy's mom and dad are the best." She had her face pressed to the car window.

J.J. scanned the area beyond the pool, but she didn't recognize anyone but Mack and Benny. Thanks to the short rise on which she'd parked, they had a panoramic view of huddled men in dirty jeans and wet boots, some in plaid shirts, some shirtless, standing near the hose J.J. had left twined through one bucket. The men took turns washing off in the spray. For some reason, that irked J.J. Maybe because the three of them were here, covered in grime, their hair stiff from smoke and sweat, or maybe because the area was suffering the worst drought in years, and the men seemed to be cavorting in the water as if Mack's ranch had an endless supply.

But why should she care? It wasn't her ranch.

Mack kept looking and gesturing toward the SUV. She hoped she wasn't the topic of conversation. On second thought, why would it matter if he bad-mouthed her to other ranchers? She wouldn't be here once her job was done.

"Is it okay if Jiggs and I go down there?" Zoey asked.

That request caused J.J. a momentary panic. On the one hand, now that Mack had returned she wasn't in charge of his daughter, but on the other, shouldn't she still keep Zoey safe? "It's probably better if you and Jiggs wait here until your dad gives us the all clear, okay? See, the men are still filling buckets with water. Looks like they're going to walk the line of fire. I imagine they'll check for hot spots. There may still be embers. You don't want Jiggs to burn his paws."

Zoey petted the panting dog. "Fine. If I had his leash we could go, though. We could wait in the corral. Benny shut off the pool pump, but I bet the ground in the corral will stay wet all afternoon."

"No doubt." Personally, J.J. was glad to see things winding down. She was less jittery and her stomach had relaxed.

Erma shifted up on her good hip.

J.J. offered an expression of sympathy. "You've been a trouper, Erma. This ordeal can't have been easy. Oh, I believe the fire trucks are leaving. With the smoke dissipating," she added, "you can see the charred ground. Man, that fire must have traveled a huge distance. The ranch dodged a bullet, but not by much."

"What bullet?" Zoey piped up from the backseat.

"It's a figure of speech," Erma said. "It means we're lucky the ranch didn't burn down."

Silence descended, each of them withdrawing into themselves to contemplate the fire that they'd survived—that they'd diverted together.

Jiggs was the first to notice someone approaching the SUV. The dog bounded from side to side of the backseat, smacking his nose on the windows, filling the car with excited yips.

"Hang on to Jiggs," J.J. said, slowly cracking her door ajar and craning her neck to identify the arrival who was silhouetted against the sinking sun.

Mack grasped the door, widening the gap. His broad shoulders blocked the sun and for a drawn-out moment his gaze fused with J.J.'s. Then appearing somewhat shamefaced, he tilted his chin down and rubbed the back of his neck. The brim of his straw hat covered his guilty expression. "I, um, owe you an apology, Jill."

"You think?" she murmured.

"Yeah. Neighbors who helped fight the fire said you spotted the smoke early and phoned the dispatcher. The fire started on free-range. It might have gone unnoticed until it had too much of a head start.

A couple of the men said you ladies worked like crazy to wet the house and the barn and corral."

Zoey jumped out of the car along with Jiggs. Mack caught her around her waist and took hold of the dog's collar. "So, now you think I may have some sense?" she snapped.

Mack straightened abruptly. "You want me to grovel?"

"No. Maybe. I don't know." She faced front, flexing her sore hands. "Sometimes saying you're sorry after being hurtful isn't enough, Mack."

"I'm ashamed of you, Mackenzie," Erma said. "The corral, the barn, even the house—everything might be rubble if not for Jill."

"Yeah, Dad. I wanted to leave when Erma said it was a grass fire. J.J. made us pack some clothes and other important stuff from the house. She took the animals out of the barn, moved your pickup and then said we had to do the best we could to water as far as the hoses would reach."

"And Jill didn't stop there," Erma added. "She hauled water in buckets and dumped it around the corral posts. Heaven knows I was too rattled to think of pumping out the pool water."

"Stop." J.J. held up a hand. "What I don't understand, Mack, is why you'd believe for a minute I'd be so careless as to let us all die when I had two vehicles at my disposal. You know me. Or you used to. I assumed you'd trust my judgment when it comes to basic survival. Obviously not." Her voice broke and she had to turn away.

"I'm sorry. What else can I say?" Mack asked, a tremor in his voice, too. "Put yourself in my boots.

Benny and I saw the grass fire when we were too far out to be of help. We almost ran our horses into the ground getting here, but I expected all of you would be gone to safety. When I saw you still here…" He gestured feebly.

J.J. wiped an errant tear that slid to her chin. "Forget it. I'm too tired to process anything at the moment."

Zoey buried her face in her dad's loose shirtfront and tightened her arms around his waist. "If the fire's out, can't we all go home? I want a shower and clean clothes."

"That's the best idea I've heard so far," Erma said stoutly. "The fire must be done, if the trucks left. Our neighbors are heading out. You'd better go tell everyone thanks again, Mackenzie. Then bring your pickup home. Jill, are you up to driving us back to the house?"

She nodded, and started the engine.

"Zoey," Mack said, "do you want to ride with me or go with Jill and Erma?"

Frowning, the girl hesitated. "I'll go with you," she finally told her dad.

"Wait," J.J. called as they started off on foot, Jiggs trotting between them. "Your keys." She set the emergency brake and loosened her seat belt, ignoring her sore palm as she dug in the pocket of her shorts. She tossed the ring of keys to Mack, who caught it deftly as she settled back. "And you'd better check Jiggs, he's limping." With that she slammed her door and revved the engine.

"Forgiveness is a noble virtue," Erma said obliquely as J.J. backed up and turned her vehicle around.

J.J. fixed the older woman with an unrepentant stare.

"I'm just saying," Erma went on, "that holding on to a grudge won't make you feel better."

"I've done nothing wrong. Mack's the one who should feel guilty."

"He does."

"Really?"

Erma bobbed her head. "I don't stand by what he said, but I've known him since he was a boy. He gets most defensive when he's hurt. I honestly have no idea what happened to end your engagement. He's harbored pain from it all these years."

"I doubt that. Uh, can we change the subject, please?" J.J. parked at the house and shut off the engine. "I didn't want to take this job, but the staff picked Mack to be featured in the August issue. It's just a coincidence that we have a history. The magazine had one photographer off on assignment and our part-timer out on maternity leave. I came because there was no one else. Your accident altered my plans a bit. But when my job is finished I'm out of here. I'm sure Mack doesn't want to dredge up our past, and neither do I."

Erma unbuckled her seat belt and opened her door. "As you wish, dear. I'm just an old lady, but I think I've learned to read people pretty well. I sense you still have issues with how you two left things. But I'm wise enough to know when I've said my piece. Right now I believe Zoey was right... Showers are what we all need. Will you bring the wheelchair, Jill? If you lay out some clothes and a clean towel, I'm ready to wash my cares away."

J.J. climbed out and got the wheelchair from the

back. She opened it, brought it around and helped Erma into the seat. "Erma, I shouldn't have lashed out. You were never anything but nice to me. I'm afraid the stress of today has brought out the worst in Mack and me. I apologize for growling at you."

Erma waved a blue-veined hand. "No need. You're entitled to your privacy. And the bottom line is, we all owe you a debt of gratitude. What I can't decide is this—after I clean up do I want to take a full dose of my medicine and go straight to la-la land, or did all our hard work saving the ranch make me so hungry I'll delay bed for food?"

J.J. laughed as she wheeled Erma into the house and straight to her room. "I guess what they say about women's work never being done truly applies here. Mack and Benny had planned to arrive in time for lunch, so they'll probably be starved. Let's get cleaned up. Then we can put our heads together and figure out something to serve with that Jell-O salad."

"Now don't get all huffy, Jill, but watching you today, I've never seen anyone who claims to be a city woman more suited to living on a ranch."

J.J. paused in the act of putting Erma's soap and shampoo within easy reach. "I'll take that as a compliment," she said, adjusting the water to warm. She looped a towel and washcloth over the shower rod. Helping Erma stand, J.J. gave her a little hug. "Just between us, Erma, I'm over my snit."

Erma smiled. "You're allowed a few snits."

"After I shower I'll bring in the bags we packed. That is, if Mack and Zoey don't beat me to it."

"They may. There's really nothing wrong with demanding some perks from a groveling man. Stuff like that strengthens his soul."

J.J. went to lay out Erma's clothes, again wishing forgiveness was as simple as Erma seemed to think.

Chapter Eight

J.J. stripped out of her filthy, smoky clothes. She wondered if they'd ever wash clean. She shook out a plastic bag that held a shirt she'd bought in the airport on the way here, rolled her dirty clothes into a ball, stuffed them in and tied the top. Then she turned on the shower. The moment she stepped under the spray she felt refreshed, but the hot water stung her cuts. Both arms and her hands were scratched, as were both knees and one shin. She remembered hitting the shin while leading the horses to the creek.

She felt the injuries on her palms the most as she shampooed her hair. But it still felt good to make her hair clean and silky again. Then she felt a dip in water pressure and figured Mack and Zoey had come in and gone to shower. J.J. rushed what she would have liked to be leisurely. Aware of how much water they'd pumped out of Mack's wells today, she did a quick rinse. Because the hot, late-afternoon sun still streamed through the windows that flanked the patio, she donned a pair of clean running shorts and a matching T-shirt. It hurt her hands to braid her wet hair so she toweled it and left it to dry naturally. She found salve in the medicine cabinet and rubbed some into the cuts.

Afraid she'd spent too much time on herself and that perhaps Erma needed her, J.J. flung open the door to the patio and hurried across to the housekeeper's room. She was surprised when Mack unfolded his long body from where he lounged against the side wall. His hair, too, was still damp from his shower and curled over his forehead and ears.

"I knocked, but I guess you didn't hear me," he said by way of an opening.

Still cataloging how good he looked and savoring his fresh, citrusy masculine scent, J.J. said nothing.

"Hell, I wouldn't blame you if you knocked me upside the head," he muttered, messing up his hair with one hand. "Zoey filled me in on everything you did, rescuing the barn animals and saving important items from the house. Then, even with that fire approaching, you strung hoses and soaked the perimeter of the property, probably saving my barn. I can never repay you, Jill." Mack's expression underscored the truth of his words.

"I don't expect repayment. This ranch is a treasure. I remember how proud you always were of your family's history. I couldn't bear to think that it might be lost."

"Thank you, Jill. If the tables were turned—"

She made a sweeping brush with one hand. "Today I learned that it's impossible to prejudge how I'd operate in a crisis until I actually faced one. Another time, under different circumstances I might be totally incompetent. This afternoon, I went on instinct. I saved pictures because they're important to me. For all I know, you may never find the horses I turned out at the river. Or the mama cow and her calf, and they're probably worth more than old photo albums."

"You can quit worrying. Benny already caught Misty and Splash. I'm sure he has the heifer and her calf by now, too. The chickens are scattered all the hell over the place, though. We'll probably have to lure them back with a trail of corn." It was clear that Mack was trying not to laugh in spite of everything.

"They weren't in danger, it turned out. I wasted time there." J.J. shook her head.

"If the barn had caught, and you hadn't opened their pen, the entire flock would have been barbe-cued."

"Oh, yuck! My stomach's still in turmoil and you're cracking macabre jokes." J.J. frowned at him. "I'd forgotten that about you, Mack. Making jokes is how you deal with catastrophe."

He sobered at once. "Is that why you—"

Erma shoved open the door from her room with a loud bang. She was in her wheelchair but didn't look totally put together. "Are you two carping at each other again?"

"I'm trying to apologize," Mack said.

"Oh, well, I didn't hear what either of you were say-ing, but it's good you're finally making up."

J.J. rushed past Mack. She bent down, her expres-sion contrite. "Mack waylaid me when I was com-ing to your room. Let me take you back in. You have your T-shirt on inside out. Why didn't you call for me to help you?"

"Inside out?" Erma pulled at the fabric and crossed her eyes in an attempt to see the shoulder seams. "Honest to Pete. I've been dressing myself for nearly seventy years. You'd think I'd injured my noggin instead of my hip."

J.J. offered a smile. "I'm impressed you got in and out of the shower without assistance. That proves you're feeling better."

"Maybe not," Erma said, raising her voice so that Mack could hear. "I just checked the answering machine. Yesterday, the orthopedic doctor from Lubbock phoned and left a message. He said the radiologist thinks I may have a hairline fracture of the…something-something bone. He says he needs X-rays from a different angle, and wants me to have them done Tuesday by the radiologist in Lubbock, the guy our E.R. doctor sent my films to." She sighed heavily. "I'm more darned trouble than I'm worth."

"Nonsense!" Mack strode over to where Erma sat. "I'll take you. Call him back and see when they can fit you in. Trevor and Eldon will be riding in tomorrow once the herd has settled into the summer pasture. We'll need to check the fences to see if we lost any posts in the fire, but the men can do that without me."

"I thought you and Jill were going to ride out to the summer range so she could take pictures of you with the cattle, Mack."

J.J. shushed Erma. "I can drive you to Lubbock," she volunteered. "While you're at your appointment, I'll run by and see my mother. If she's not too busy with her social calendar, that is," J.J. added.

Zoey bounded out from the living room onto the flagstone patio. "I want to go to Lubbock. After J.J. visits her mom, maybe me and her can go to the mall and shop for my school clothes."

"*She and I* can go to the mall," Mack chided,

settling the galloping girl with a firm hand on her shoulder.

"You want to go school shopping?" Zoey gaped.

Mack gave an inelegant snort. "Knock it off. You know good grammar."

"What kid uses good grammar except in class?"

"You'd be the first," Erma said.

Mack's gaze skipped from his daughter to J.J. "I don't object to all of us going but, Zoey, it's too early to shop for next year's school clothes. You always shoot up a foot over the summer. It makes no sense to buy things you'll outgrow by September."

Zoey's face crumpled. "But J.J. won't be here then to help me pick out clothes! Daddy, she let me wear some of her stuff this morning when she took my pictures. Wait till you see how cool I looked. I won't outgrow accessories or…or eye shadow."

Mack's scowl settled on J.J. "I thought I said…"

"You said you didn't want her duded up. There's such thing as the tasteful use of eye shadow and lip gloss, Mack."

"She doesn't need eye shadow or other goo on her face."

"Daddy!" Zoey cried. "Most of my friends already use makeup. And next year I'll be in junior high." She stomped a foot. "You just don't want me to grow up, but I am, and I want to fit in."

Mack's mouth opened and closed a couple of times.

J.J. came to his rescue, although she considered letting him swing. "Zoey, we talked about how some girls go overboard with makeup. Your dad doesn't want you making mistakes he's seen some other girls make."

"I'm not sure if that's what I meant, but it sounds right," he said, spreading his hands.

"Lord have mercy," Erma muttered. "It's a fact nobody in this household knows anything about buying or using makeup. Mackenzie, we can't hide our heads in the sand forever. After Jill did Zoey's hair this morning, I could see she's plumb outgrown her tomboy phase. Can't you just thank Jill? She's bailed us out in more than one way."

Mack threw up his hands. "I'm outnumbered. We'll talk about this later."

J.J. knew when to walk away with a small victory. Mack hadn't said no to letting Zoey spread her wings a little. So, when she saw the girl preparing to press her dad further, she caught Zoey's eye and wagged a cautionary finger. "While Erma calls her doctor, let's you and I bring back the stuff we put in your dad's pickup. Then we'll help her figure out something to make for supper."

Zoey swallowed what she might have said, instead agreeing cheerily. "You bet. Do you think there might be time before supper for you to put my hair in that halo braid? I took it down to wash the smoke out of my hair, but I want Daddy to see how nice it looks. He saw me when he got home, but he was so upset about the fire he didn't really *see* me. Know what I mean?"

J.J. nodded. "If we go shopping tomorrow, I'll look for a style book that shows step-by-step a number of ways to braid your hair."

"Cool."

Laughing, J.J. hooked her arm through Zoey's and the two struck out across the patio toward Mack's pickup.

MACK WATCHED THEM leave—two slender women not so different in height as he would have thought. Zoey was growing up before his eyes.

As for Jill, as he watched the sway of her hips, his hands itched to explore her body the way he once had.

Erma cleared her throat. "It's easy to see what you *really* think about Jill, Mackenzie. Can you answer me this? Why do you constantly rag on her?"

Mack had forgotten that Erma was still sitting in the doorway. He tried not to sound guilty when he blustered, "I was thinking I've missed the boat when it comes to admitting that Zoey's not a little girl anymore."

"Right, that's what you were thinking. I'm old, but I'm not feebleminded. You don't want Jill to catch you lollygagging around with that moon-calf look. Wheel me into the kitchen so I can use the phone. I'm learning to operate this danged chair on my own, but after holding a hose as long as I did, I'd appreciate you doing the work right now."

"No problem. You only have to ask." Grasping the handles of the wheelchair, Mack circled it around and took the closer route to the kitchen through Erma's room.

"Mackenzie, I rarely stick my nose into your private life. Lord knows I wanted to ask why you and Jill broke up, and why instead of going after her you took up with Faith straightaway. She was never the right woman for you."

Mack moved the wheelchair into the alcove in jerky steps. "Your decision to stay out of my personal life was best," he said, turning cool.

"Bah!" Erma reached back and smacked his rigid

arm. "You're allowed to admit you messed up. The world doesn't have to know. Not even Zoey."

"What are you talking about?" Mack stopped short of the kitchen counter.

"You think I don't know how soon Faith left your bed and took up residence in the room we turned into Zoey's nursery? I know when love cools. Benny does, too. What apparently escaped you, Mackenzie, is that you don't have to pay for a mistake forever. It's not too late to grab some happiness. You deserve it, and the woman capable of giving it to you has dropped back into your life. That's luck, plain and simple."

Mack felt as if he'd been hit in the gut with a two-by-four. He'd honestly believed that he'd succeeded in hiding the sad state of his marriage from the two people who knew him best. Now, he felt panic welling. He had battled Faith's parents in court once when they claimed they should have the right to raise their dead daughter's baby. They were religious zealots, but they weren't stupid. Rumors had a way of circulating in small towns. If he took up with Jill, and Erma, Benny or anyone so much as hinted that he loved Jill years ago, well, the Reverend Bode Adams would probably have him back in court so fast his head would spin. He hadn't loved Faith the way she deserved, but he had promised he'd never allow her parents to raise her baby. That was a promise he intended to keep.

"Well, Erma, maybe you should have asked me back then instead of building romantic fantasies in your head. Faith's heart was so damaged from childhood rheumatic fever that her OB/GYN advised her to terminate her pregnancy. Faith refused, and her cardiologist said her only hope of carrying a baby to term was to follow a strict regimen he and her OB/GYN set up. Frequent naps, no bending, lifting or stretching. That's why you got stuck with all the cooking and housekeeping. Another of the doctor's orders was that we cease, uh, you know." Mack reached for the phone as he stumbled over what was really the truth. "I put the single bed in the room off the master suite and I moved Faith's things because of that. We hoped her heart would withstand an early caesarean section if she followed orders to a T. You know the rest—she went into early labor and the doctors were lucky to save Zoey. So, now can we leave all this in the past?"

Erma twisted in her seat and gave him the evil eye. "We don't have to speak of that time again. But none of that, then or now, precludes you from opening your heart and your life to another woman. It's time, Mackenzie."

"What if I don't want to?" he flared.

She all but cackled at the notion as she pulled the specialist's card from her pocket and dialed the weekend number. "Lie to yourself if you want. One thing about your eyes, they've always shown your true feelings. So don't look at Jill while you're spouting such nonsense." Erma turned and spoke to whoever had answered her call, and Mack hastily withdrew.

Erma had needled him before, but this time what really got to him was when she'd said that he had a right to happiness—happiness that included having a woman in his life. It was true that for the past few years Erma had pushed him to find a wife, pointing out that she was getting older and that chores piled up faster than she could get to them. Or she'd say Zoey would benefit from having a younger woman around. Not once in his recollection had she made it about *his* needs.

He hadn't been a monk over the past thirteen years. But he'd been very, very discreet in choosing women to take out to dinner or a movie. None lived in La Mesa, and he'd never strung any of them along. He made it clear up front that he wasn't looking for a long-term relationship. The lawsuit Bode Adams and his wife had lodged against him when Zoey was six months old had terrified him—what if they portrayed him as a womanizer who was a bad influence on his daughter? He couldn't risk losing her, so it had taken a long time for him to look twice at any woman. Added to that stress, the lawsuit had nearly bankrupted him when he'd still been trying to get the hang of running the ranch without his dad. Benny had pulled his fat out of the fire and taught him how to be a responsible rancher. Otherwise, Turkey Creek Ranch might have gone under. Only Benny and the banker in town, who knew and respected Mack's father, were aware of how close he'd come to losing everything. His love life had never been a high priority.

Until he walked into that library, saw Jill and was tossed into a sea of memories. Sweet memories of a carefree time before one bad thing after another had struck.

So why had he come away from the library feeling so angry? He'd been nothing but cantankerous since—far from how he felt inside anytime he ran into Jill. Like the night on the patio when he couldn't help but kiss her.

And not ten minutes ago Erma had caught him salivating over the idea of hauling Jill off to his bedroom.

He adjusted the loose-fitting cargo shorts he'd thrown on after his shower. Come to think of it, where were all his blue jeans? There hadn't been any in his closet.

As he waited for Erma to finish her call, the front door opened and he heard a melding of girlish and womanly laughter. Zoey and Jill came down the hall. They were both weighed down by piles of stuff.

"Hey, do either of you need help?" he called, then was sorry to acknowledge how quickly their laughter died.

"We're bringing back everything we dragged out to your pickup," Jill said.

"Oh, I see you have some things from my closet." He untangled eight or so hangers from Jill's left arm. "And you have the bedspread my mother crocheted. It was one of my dad's most prized possessions, but he never used it on his bed."

Jill handed it to him and smiled. "I only knew it was handmade, old and irreplaceable. When Erma saw me with it, she said it was one of the few things you have of your mom's."

Erma wheeled into the hall. "It's something you'll want to put in Zoey's hope chest, Mackenzie."

"What's a hope chest?" Zoey asked. She had one foot on the stairs that led to the second story. Turning back to face the others, she dropped a pillow and a stuffed lamb that had been perched atop the photo albums and frames she carried.

"Most kids don't have them anymore," Jill said, shaking her bangs out of her eyes.

Erma looked up at Zoey. "In my day when a girl became a teen, her family would fill a cedar box with special things a new bride would need, like hand-sewn or embroidered linens, maybe silverware or china. Mothers and grandmothers taught the girls how to make handcrafts, and they all spent time sewing pretty things. Because the girls dreamed of getting married, the boxes became known as hope chests."

Mack and Zoey looked at Erma with doubt.

"What? Neither of you has heard of hope chests?"

"Do you have one, J.J.?" Zoey asked.

"No. Even if moms did that in the '90s, my mother wasn't into handcrafts, which is why I find it odd that she's now immersed in a ceramics course. She dreamed of traveling, so she bought me suitcases for my high school graduation. It's just as well since mine would be more like a hopeless chest."

"Hopeless, why?" Zoey tried to peer around her dad, who had picked up the pillow and the lamb.

Mack glanced at Jill and saw sadness in her eyes before she lowered her lashes.

"If I got a dime every time you asked why, Ms. No-sybody, we'd be zillionaires," Mack said. "Upstairs with you, monkey, before you lose any more of your treasures. And go slow so you don't trip and fall," he said, nudging her upward with his elbow.

"Aw, it must have something to do with love," Zoey groused, plodding up a few steps. "I told Brandy nobody ever explains anything if it has to do with love."

"My job keeps me traveling around the world," Jill added, "it's why people would say there's no hope left."

Zoey had reached the landing and stopped. "Well, I think you can still get married if you want to, J.J." She disappeared around the bend and on into her room, leaving Mack and J.J. standing awkwardly below with Erma, who didn't try to hide her sly grin.

Jill flushed. "Um, I...had better put these things back where I found them. Then I'll help Erma make supper."

"Zoey tends not to filter what comes out of her mouth," Mack said. "I'm sure it never occurred to her that you could be dating someone in New York."

"I'm not."

He ought to let that go. "No surprise. What man could pry you away from the career and the city that's more important to you than anything else?"

"Not true. If I didn't need health benefits I could set my own hours freelancing, and I wouldn't need to work in New York City." Jill nipped in her lower lip. "But maybe that isn't what you were getting at. What were you asking, Mack?"

Standing here, face-to-face, offered the perfect opportunity to ask the question that had plagued him for so many years. But, with Erma looking on, Mack got cold feet. If the big city wasn't what drove her, then she must have left because he'd failed her somehow. "You fit in here," he said instead. "But La Mesa and Turkey Creek are a far cry from life in New York City."

"I love it here!"

"Do you?" Mack's heart sped up, even as he was bombarded with snippets of another time, when, during their college breaks, they'd stolen away to the creek to make love under a canopy of stars. At one point as they kissed, she'd leaned back and declared, *I love it here.* She'd followed up that statement with: *I love you, too, and I always will.*

Erma said, "Wasting a whole day driving me to

Lubbock'll ruin your plan to go with Jill and get photos of you with the herd, Mackenzie."

"Don't worry, Erma," Jill said. "The magazine will love a close-up of Mack with one horse and another with the single cow and her calf. I wanted to impress readers with the size of his herd, but…"

"Why would readers of a women's magazine care about the size of my herd?"

Jill shot him an expression as if he'd sprouted two heads. "Readers care about that kind of detail. But my article will cover what you do as a rancher—the number of acres you own and how much land you lease for grazing. I can also say how many head of cattle you generally run each year."

Mack shifted the clothes he held. "We still have a couple of days before you leave. We could ride out to my summer range midweek. And you said your article will include my charity work. My first meeting with the steak-fry committee chairs is coming up. You can come along if you'd like."

"I'd love to. It'll be great for the article. And when we're in Lubbock, I'd like to go to a photography shop for good photo paper and frames. Zoey wants copies of the pictures I took and I know she wants to frame at least one. Barring any other unforeseen disasters like we had today, there's no reason I can't wind everything up and still find time to get her pictures ready."

Mack didn't want to think about Jill leaving. With her here, he was reminded of so many things he missed about her. She could fill the lonely times in his life—if he could trust her. But the last thing he needed was to get involved with her again. She'd ripped out his heart before, and she wasn't thinking like him now. She seemed anxious to leave, with all her focus on photography.

"Speaking of pictures, those wooden frames you're holding are heavy," he said, suddenly ready to be on his way and have her be on hers.

Above them a door crashed open and Zoey burst out of her room. She hung over the banister. "Are you two still holding all the junk we brought out of the pickup?"

"We've been talking," Mack said.

"About what? I put away everything I took up to my room."

"Scheduling," Jill said. "Like the trip to Lubbock."

Zoey brightened and skipped down the stairs. "So, Daddy, can J.J. *please* take me shopping for some school clothes? I only have a half day at school tomorrow and then I'm out till seventh grade."

Mack sucked in a breath. "Jill mentioned going to a special store to buy paper to print your photos. And she said you wanted frames. They have those at the general store, you know. How do you know what size you need for a photo you haven't even seen? And what if none Jill took are good?"

"Daddy!" Zoey sounded annoyed. "J.J. is world-famous. Of course they'll be good."

"Excuse me." Now he answered in a tone that was dust dry. "I forgot we've been graced by such a grand and exalted photographer."

"World-famous," Zoey repeated.

Jill flushed. "Knock it off. We were having a civilized conversation for a change. Maybe you'd like to tell me what about my work needles you, Mack. As I recall, you used to be proud of me. Well, of my skill as a photographer, I mean."

Mack saw Zoey's head swivel between him and Jill. She was far too interested in the exchange—as was Erma. He was only too aware of how attached they'd both gotten to Jill in a few short days. Since Jill dropped into their lives, it was clear that from Zoey's perspective Jill could give the kind of attention his daughter craved. He knew from experience the pain that followed when Jill walked away, cutting off the warmth and love she so freely lavished.

"Zoey, help Jill hang the pictures in the hall. I'm taking these things to my room and then I'll find Benny and make sure that there are no hot spots left along the fire line before it gets dark."

He disappeared so fast, J.J. had to blink. She handed Zoey two old photo albums to put on the shelf in the living room, then rehung the wedding photos of Mack's family in their proper order along the hall. She wished she had asked about the absence of his wedding pictures while he'd been in a good mood. Maybe their pictures had been terrible. Was that why he had it in for her occupation? She'd known wedding disasters to happen. Not to her, but a few times she'd been asked to salvage botched takes of the most important event in a couple's life. Did that describe Mack's wedding? Botched?

No, that was mean. Just because she and Mack had planned to have their simple wedding right here at the ranch didn't give her the right to think badly of the wedding he'd had with Faith instead. So often she'd imagined herself walking down—no, floating down—that lovely old staircase. But she had planned to float down in the beautiful, long gown she'd bought after he proposed—and straight into Mack's arms. Her mother, at her authorization, had sold that gown in a garage sale after Rex died. J.J. would have never worn the dress to marry anyone but Mack.

J.J. straightened the frame that held the photo of Mack's mom and dad. He was blessed with a lot of his mother's fine features. Scanning the other photos, J.J. saw bits of Mack in all of them. But nothing of Zoey. The shape of her face, the color of her hair and eyes were...different. Obviously Faith's family genes had overridden the Bannermans' most prominent hallmarks. Shrugging, she turned to Erma, who was waiting in the hall. "Okay, let's go see what we can throw together for the evening meal."

Chapter Nine

Tuesday morning, a hot sun splashed across the shiny
ribbon of asphalt that led to Lubbock, and heat dev-
ils shimmered above dry cotton fields that flanked
the highway. Mack and Erma sat in the front of the
pickup. Before they left the ranch Erma tried to get
Jill to sit up front. She refused politely, instead shar-
ing the backseat with Zoey, who filled the cab with
chatter. "I wish Brandy could have come today, but
she's helping her mom at the produce stand. J.J., do
you think any of the mall stores will have a jacket like
the one you let me wear for my photographs?"

Her dad broke in, "Zoey, why don't you call her
Jill? It's her name. And it sounds a lot prettier."

She made a face at him in his mirror. "J.J. is different. Classier," Zoey went on as if her dad hadn't
chided her. "Do you think I can find a hat kinda like
yours? It's so cool. Brandy said hats are totally in
right now, and everyone will be wearing them when
school starts. Do you want me to call you, Jill? You
introduced yourself to Brandy and me as J.J. We think
using initials is way…chic."

"Zoey!" This time there was no mistaking the firm-
ness in Mack's warning.

J.J. laughed. "It's okay, Mack. I answer to either. A dozen years ago when I started shopping my portfolio around, going by initials was in vogue and a lot of women did it."

"When I was little," Erma said, "most women could only be teachers or nurses if they wanted a career. A handful became doctors or lawyers. They didn't have it easy, because those jobs were considered men's domain. Careers for women are wide-open today."

"Yep," Zoey said. "My teachers say girls can have any career we choose. Some even want us to know what we want to be right now! How can we? Brandy changes her mind a lot, and gosh, college is a long way off."

J.J. smiled at Zoey. "It's good you're planning on college."

"I have to. My dad set me up a college fund at Texas Tech."

"Ah, a prepaid tuition plan. That's smart. But you don't sound too happy," J.J. said, catching and holding Mack's gaze for a moment in his rearview mirror.

"Brandy said maybe I'll want to go to some other college. She wants to go to the university her mom and dad went to in Utah. And we kinda want to go together."

Mack glanced back at her. "Tell Brandy you'll graduate without college debt hanging over your head. I started this 529 fund when you were five, Zoey. I locked in the rate of tuition for that year. Do you have any idea how much tuition climbs each year?"

She shook her head.

"A lot," J.J. said. "Believe me, you'll appreciate your father's foresight when your friends are saddled with debt. I had scholarships and a discount because my stepdad taught at Tech. But I had to borrow to pay room and board in Paris for my postgraduate work. It was pricy and I only paid off my loans a couple of years ago."

Zoey propped her elbows on her knees and set her chin in her hands. "All I'm thinking about now is getting through junior high."

The three adults in the vehicle burst out laughing. Mack winked at J.J., and for a split second his gaze in the mirror settled on her mouth. She was surprised by the sudden heat that rose inside her. Like old times she felt drawn to him. Then a gust of wind kicked up dust across the highway, and Mack returned his attention to the road.

But J.J. knew he'd felt it, too, by the way he cleared his throat and the catch in his voice. "What time is your mom expecting you, Jilly?"

Jilly. That gave her goose bumps. "I didn't set a time. I figured we'd see how long they think Erma will be at her appointment. Then I'll take a cab to the retirement center."

"Take a cab?" Mack drawled. "This is Lubbock, remember. Don't they only have cabs at the airport?"

"How long since you've been up here?" J.J. asked. "Lubbock's grown. They even have great internet and digital cell service now."

"I'll be a while," Erma said. "I have to see the orthopedic doctor and have X-rays. The nurse said the doctor wants me to wait while he has someone read the films, since we're from out of town."

Mack checked his watch. "Your appointment's at nine. You'll probably be tied up until lunch at least.

Jill, are you going for a quick visit or spending the day with Bonnie? Zoey and I can drive you there and wait."

"Don't be silly. Come in with me and say hello. I wasn't planning to stay long. For one thing she hasn't jumped for joy at the prospect of seeing me this visit. When I came to help her move she was so depressed and needy. I should be glad she's gotten active, but…" Her voice trailed off, and she found Mack studying her again in the mirror. Mack Bannerman had the most expressive eyes of any person J.J. had ever met—and she worked with models who used every asset to express emotion to her camera. But his gaze now made her feel compelled to add, "I'm happy for her, though. Her world used to revolve around Rex."

"True," Mack agreed. "And I shouldn't pass judgment even though your mother was never a fan of me. I didn't know either of your folks that well."

"She didn't like you because you were in my corner and didn't bend over backward for her."

Back then, things had been especially volatile between her and her mother. In fact, J.J. had met Mack the very day she'd learned Rex wasn't her real dad. It came to light when she was signing up for classes. Rex had gotten her a special reduced tuition rate afforded to children of employees, but on the form he noted that he'd never adopted her. Terribly upset, she had confronted her mom, who confessed J.J.'s biological dad had been an alcoholic who had died a few years before in prison where he was serving time for negligent homicide. J.J. felt duped—deceived—despite the fact that Rex had been a good father. They had lied to her. Bonnie refused to admit she'd done anything wrong. J.J. went crying back to college and met Mack in the parking lot. He heard her sobbing her heart out and came to see if she needed rescuing.

Four years later he betrayed her with Faith. That betrayal drilled the same kind of hole in her heart as her mother's lie had. Returning to Lubbock now with Mack, preparing to visit her mom, sent J.J. cartwheeling back into dark reflections of those painful times. Very probably Mack knew, because he shifted his eyes away from her, and even adjusted the rearview mirror.

They reached the clinic, where Erma's doctor and radiologist both practiced. "I'll go in with Erma and see what's what. Are you two okay waiting out here?" Mack asked J.J. and Zoey.

"I'm good," Zoey said. "But I can't wait to go to the mall."

"Don't get too anxious. It'll be this afternoon, and only then if Erma feels up to sitting around in the food court with me while you and Jill visit a couple of stores."

"A couple?" Zoey unfastened her seat belt and slid to the edge of her seat. "Daddy, shopping can't be rushed. Can't you leave us at the mall and you guys go do something else?"

"Like what?" Mack asked. "We came to Lubbock today for Erma's appointments. Depending on if they hurt her too much with their poking and prodding, she may want to go straight home."

Zoey flopped back in her seat. "Then can J.J. bring me here again before she goes back to New York? Maybe Brandy can come, too." Leaning forward, she looked more hopeful.

Her dad, who'd taken Erma's wheelchair out of the

pickup bed, spoke to Zoey this time through Erma's open door. "By the way, last night Benny confirmed that his cousin Sonja will arrive today. I thought maybe tomorrow I'd take Jill and ride out to the summer pasture. It *is* why she's here, Zoey."

"Bro...ther!" Zoey slumped again.

"Mackenzie, you need to give them some time to shop," Erma said as he helped her out of the truck. "I'll take a pain pill if need be."

"Oh, right." Mack huffed out a harsh breath. "We've all seen how fast those painkillers knock you out. How long does it take for Zoey to buy jeans and a few shirts?"

Erma remained firm. "I'll be fine. Haven't you been listening? Zoey wants Jill to help her pick out something other than her usual clothes." Erma said something else, but Mack shut the door, cutting off whatever she added.

"You should have asked Dad for his keys, J.J. We could go to the mall right now. You heard him, right? He still expects me to dress like a cowboy."

"The mall doesn't open until ten. Relax, Zoey. Why don't you make a list of top priority items? I'm sure your dad will let you buy a nice skirt or two, and feminine tops. If we can carve out an hour and go straight to the departments on your list, I know we can choose a few nice pieces for your fall wardrobe. Remember, though, most of the stores will have just stocked their summery things."

"Oh, bummer. I want a jacket like yours, and a hat."

"It still helps to make a list, and even note colors to mix and match. That way you don't get distracted by pretty things that won't go with anything else in your wardrobe."

"Great idea! I've never done anything like that. Neither has Brandy, I bet, 'cause she gets her mom to take stuff back all the time. Oh, if only you could come back before school starts. Better yet, don't go back to New York."

"You know that's not possible, Zoey. But maybe we can keep in touch. If you have questions about clothes you can ask me."

The girl looked glum. "My dad's strict about me using his computer. He's a worrywart, afraid for what he hears about kids on social media. I at least want a cell phone. I doubt I'll get one. Brandy thinks she'll get one for her birthday. It's before school starts. Maybe she'll let me text you. Do you text?"

J.J. nodded. "Here comes your dad. That didn't take long."

He opened the driver's door and stuck his head in. "Jill, can you program your cell number into my phone? I'll leave it with Erma, then we can go. If we stop by your mom's and then head to the mall, you and Zoey can get your shopping done. Erma will call you if she finishes early. The receptionist guessed it'll be until twelve or twelve-thirty. If you two are shopped out by then we can pick Erma up and eat on the way out of town."

"Daddy, I love you, but I'll never be shopped out." Zoey's laughter mingled with J.J.'s.

"Wrong," he said, taking his phone back from J.J. "If I give you cash instead of handing over my debit card I can curtail your time."

Zoey's face fell.

Grinning, Mack left after giving J.J. a conspiratorial wink that again made her heart squeeze. Her cell phone chimed and she almost dropped it. Startled, she answered without checking who was calling. "Hello?"

Mack's deep voice shook her further, but he only said, "Just checking to make sure Erma can reach you."

"You think I'd program in a phony number? Sheesh!" She hung up, and seconds later Mack came out of the building and strode to the pickup, whistling.

"You two aren't gonna make me chauffeur, are you?"

"J.J., you sit up front." Zoey nudged her.

"Why me? It's you who needs to butter him up for your trip to the mall."

"Jill, come on up here," Mack said, revving the engine. "I need you to direct me to your mom's new place."

She climbed out, buckled into Erma's spot, then rattled off the directions.

Mack said, "Whoa. Whoa. I don't know the streets of Lubbock as well as you do."

"Sorry." She spoke slower and gave specific streets. "This is it," she said a short while later, directing Mack to park in an area marked for visitors. "Nine-twenty," she murmured. "I hope we catch Mom before she's off to Tai Chi or something."

"Sure you want us to tag along?" Mack swept a glance over the resortlike complex. "Should you call and warn her you're barging in with other people?"

Zoey had already jumped out and slammed her door. "You said we didn't have to stay long, right?"

"We'll say hi, and ask if Mom wants to come with

us to the mall. My mother is the queen of marathon shopping."

Mack locked the truck and followed Jill and Zoey down a walkway that led past an elaborate fountain. "Nice place," he said.

"It is. Mom's unit is there between the rec center and across from one of the two pools." She stopped in front of one of the many red-orange doors, took a deep breath and rapped soundly.

They heard a chair scrape across the floor, then the door swung inward. J.J.'s mother peered out, put a hand to her chest and said Jill's name twice, followed by, "Oh, my, I expected you to call before coming, dear. And who's this?" Bonnie Walker frowned at the girl glued to J.J.'s shoulder.

"Zoey Bannerman, Mackenzie's daughter. You remember Mack?" J.J. asked, indicating the looming presence behind her.

Her mother had on a brightly colored caftan. Red painted toenails peeked out from open-toed sandals. Her blond hair was swept back behind an ear from which dangled a large, gold hoop earring that she twisted nervously. J.J. soon understood her mom's agitation when a big, half-naked man stepped up behind Bonnie.

"Hello," he said, gesturing with a steaming coffee mug. "Did I hear Bonnie call you Jill? Nice to meet you." To Bonnie, he said, "Should I give you all your privacy?" He placed the coffee in Bonnie's hand and wrapped her other around the mug to hold it steady.

Bonnie Walker's mouth opened and closed, but it was J.J. who spoke. "We, uh, are headed to the mall to shop for Zoey, and thought you might like to join us."

She cleared her throat. "I did mention that I wanted to drop by today when I called you last night. I said we were bringing Erma Fairweather to see a doctor here."

Bonnie gave her daughter the stink eye. "I'm positive you never mentioned that your business trip had anything to do with getting back together with your old college flame."

J.J. scrubbed two fingers between furrowed eyebrows. "I probably didn't tell you because you were always in a rush to get off the phone. Mack actually is the job. It's too involved to go into now, but I'm photographing him at his ranch for the magazine. Listen, Zoey is anxious to get to the mall. I'm in La Mesa until Sunday. I'll phone before I leave. Perhaps we can meet at the airport." J.J. began backing away and stepped squarely on Mack's boot.

He steadied her. "Bonnie," he said, giving a curt nod. "You don't look a day older than when last we met... What was it? Some fourteen years ago?" He smiled at Bonnie's gentleman friend, who stuck close to her. "Sorry, we didn't catch your name," Mack said, holding out a hand to shake.

The man's eyes twinkled. "Arne. Arne Biddle. I teach art at Tech and moonlight giving beginning painting classes to other seniors around the area. I bought a unit here in anticipation of retiring next year. Bonnie is my newest, most talented student." He shook Mack's hand before settling his palm with familiarity on the back of Bonnie's slender neck. "I'm sure we'll all meet again," he said, dropping a lingering smile on J.J.'s mother and coaxing a loving one from her in return.

"Sure," was all J.J. said quickly, hustling Zoey away from the unit as she hurried back the way they'd come.

"That was…awkward," she ground out to Mack, who rushed to catch up with her.

"Why didn't we go in?" Zoey asked.

"Jill's mother already had company, and we only stopped to see if Bonnie wanted to join us at the mall," he said smoothly. Unlocking his pickup he boosted Zoey in. But as J.J. headed to the passenger's side, he took her arm and stopped her at the back of the pickup. "Are you okay?" he asked, gently brushing her hair away from her face.

"Was that man parading around my mother's condo in nothing but pajama bottoms?" Her query came out on a hissed breath.

"They could have been surgical scrubs. Maybe that's what he paints in."

"Right! You are so full of it, Bannerman."

"Your mother and Arne are well past the age of consent. What has you so upset?" He ran his hands from her shoulders to her wrists and gripped her hand.

J.J. curled her fingers around his. "Rex has barely been dead six months. My mother claimed to be devastated. And now, now…" She broke off and tugged her fingers loose.

"Your mother's not like you, Jill. You used to say she needed a man to feel like her life was complete. And hasn't she always been a lot about herself?"

"Yes. Thank you for bringing this into perspective, Mack. I guess Arne seemed pleasant enough."

"Hey," Zoey called, sticking her head out of the

back door. "What's taking you guys so long? Are we going to the mall or what?"

Mack looked guilty and J.J. laughed. "Like I said, thanks. I should be ecstatic that Arne is gainfully employed. Mom's never worked outside the home and this place costs more than Rex's pension can cover. I subsidize her. If whatever's going on with Arne works out, maybe I can—" She stopped abruptly, not wanting to let on to Mack that she wasn't totally thrilled working for *Her Own Woman*. "Anyway, let's go to the mall," she said, scooting around Mack.

He was slower to react, but Zoey's second call spurred him to get in the truck.

A short while later, outside a mall that didn't appear too busy, Mack found a parking spot halfway between the two anchor department stores. "I'm going to go find some coffee. You ladies do your thing." He pulled his wallet out of his back pocket, took out his debit card and gave it to J.J. "Do you want me to write my pin number down?"

She took the card but didn't tuck it into her purse. "How much do you want Zoey to spend?"

"Whatever it takes to get what she wants, which I gathered from Erma isn't the usual jeans and shirts." He looked to Zoey as if for clarification.

J.J. frowned at him even though Zoey danced about saying, "Yay!"

"Mack, you need to set her a dollar limit." Ignoring his shrug and Zoey's frantic attempts to silence her, J.J. said, "Setting an amount will make Zoey shop wiser, plus she'll appreciate more the art of buying items on sale."

She paused while Mack reached around her and

opened the mall door. He'd donned a light gray Stetson when he exited the truck, and he tipped it forward now, shadowing eyes similar in color to the felt brim. "I don't know a thing about the price of women's, er, girls' clothes. I can quote the price of beef on the hoof, and can gauge futures so I know when to sell my herd for top dollar, but I leave buying Zoey's clothes to Erma. She charges everything at the general store and I pay the bill. Frankly, I like it like that."

J.J. poked him in the chest with his debit card. "Forget escaping to drink coffee, mister. Erma admitted to me that she doesn't know squat about what teenagers are wearing. As the single parent of a soon-to-be teen, you need to learn what's good and what's not."

Zoey heaved a sigh. "I bet he won't like anything I want."

"Give your dad some credit. Besides, the man who pays needs to know what his money is buying. Not that I think you'd buy trashy stuff, Zoey. But it's a parent's job to have the final say."

Mack slapped his hat against his thigh, which made J.J. smile. She recognized it as a sign of nerves, something Mack did when he was out of his element.

She tucked his debit card into the breast pocket of his Western-style shirt and dragged him over to the mall directory. She read off stores listed under women's wear and finally tapped her finger on one.

Zoey's eyes lit up. "Brandy's mom just bought her some clothes from there. Heather Reed, who says I dress like a boy, bragged since last year that her mom lets her and her sister buy skirts and tops there."

"Have you got your list? It's a good place to start," J.J. said.

Mack groaned, but followed them. They entered a brightly lit store with blaring music and rounder after rounder of clothing. He shuddered. "This is torture, you know," he said, bending close to J.J.'s ear. "If this is current music, I'm way out of touch."

Zoey, who'd been gazing around as if mesmerized, said, "This is a new group, Daddy. Brandy loves them, but I only like a few of their songs."

"Thank heaven," Mack muttered.

J.J. searched through a row of skirts. She pulled out a hanger and held it up to Zoey. "This is perfect for fall. It'll look great with tights in all colors. You'll want to match tights to whatever top you wear."

"If I had a gray jacket like yours, would it look good with this?"

"I think so," J.J. said. "I'm not seeing anything in wool. You may have to come back at the end of summer."

"Come back?" Mack stopped twirling his hat. "Do they have a catalog?"

J.J. patted his chest. "You're doing fine. We've been here ten whole minutes and you haven't hyperventilated yet."

Mack followed the soft sway of Jill's hips as she wove between racks and stopped to inspect an olive-green shirt with a black panther on the front that Zoey held up. The cat's eyes glittered. Mack could tell she really wanted the shirt. And dang it, he wanted her to have it. Jill, though, didn't automatically agree just because Zoey wore her heart on her sleeve. Jill read an inside label and made Zoey read it, too. She held the shirt up to Zoey and had her look in one of the store's many mirrors. Jill draped it over a pair of shorts, in-

sisting Zoey eye both critically. Finally, Jill went to a
bin filled with socks, tights and leggings. Only after
apparently finding a pair of tights that suited them did
Jill add the top to Zoey's pile of clothes to try on, and
Mack slowly released the breath he'd been holding. He
should be paying attention to Jill's method, because
he'd have bought Zoey anything her heart desired.

He watched them repeat the process with a pair
of black, skinny jeans and camouflage jacket they
plucked from a sale rack. Still standing off to one side,
Mack heard Zoey squeal in delight when she spotted
a hanging fixture of hats. Cowboy hats were all Mack
knew, but nary a cowboy hat sat among the startlingly
large display. Zoey tried on several before choosing
two. He straightened, trying to look alive when Jill
directed Zoey to find him.

"I want both of these, but J.J. said I only need one
in black. I can't decide between them. Which do you
like best, Daddy?" She tried on one and did a pirou-
ette, then the other.

"They both look good," Mack ventured. "I'm not
used to seeing you wear any headgear but your straw
cowboy hat." He noticed Jill watching him expec-
tantly. *Damn, he didn't want to fall short here.* "The
way you're wearing your hair today, Zoey, I'd choose
the corduroy one that resembles a golfer's hat."

She sighed. "J.J. picked it, too. So, do you like my
hair like this? J.J. let me borrow her curling iron this
morning. Can I get one? She says they're cheapest at
a drugstore."

Jill walked over to them then. "We need to wind
down and check out. Erma just phoned and said she'd
be done in about half an hour. She said for us to go

ahead with our shopping, that she'd sit in the waiting room. But she sounded tired."

"Did she say what they found? Is her hip broken?"

"She said she'd tell us in person. Zoey's found some nice things, don't you think?"

He nodded.

"This'll give her a good start on her fall wardrobe. We'd talked about finding black boots, but that can wait. New styles will soon launch for fall."

Mack expected Zoey to object, but she didn't. "Daddy, will you come with me to check out? I found some bargains. J.J. said I did good."

Feeling more needed by Zoey than he had in a while, Mack happily let Jill transfer the hangers and smaller items into his arms. He couldn't help but notice their reflections in the various mirrors as they waited in line. They resembled a regular dad and mom, shopping with their daughter. Like Brandy's parents. Jill fit with him. She always had. The fact that she'd made such a hit with Zoey suggested maybe he should let the past go. He continued to mull that over as they drove out of the parking lot.

"Daddy, may I use your phone to call Brandy when you go in to get Erma?"

His daughter broke his focus on Jill. *On their starting over.*

Jill answered for him. "Your dad seems to be a million miles away, Zoey. He left his phone with Erma, remember." She snapped her fingers. "Earth to Mack," she said with a teasing smile. "Was one little ol' shopping excursion that hard on you?"

"Actually, no. I was thinking I'm starved. I hope Erma feels up to stopping for lunch."

"Me, too! Me, too," Zoey singsonged. "I could wait to eat until we get home, though, if Erma would rather. I already had the best day ever, so I don't want to be selfish."

"If there's time, I'd like to stop on the way to the clinic to pick up photo paper and a nice frame."

They did make the stop. As they traveled on to the clinic Jill explained to Zoey how to incorporate her existing wardrobe with her new purchases. Mack parked in almost the same spot he'd had earlier. "You're really growing up, Zoey," he said, climbing out of the cab. "It pleases me to hear you talk about saving money."

Jill unbuckled her seat belt and joined him outside. "Is that a tremor in your voice? Her growing up has caught you unaware, hasn't it?"

"Yeah. Hey, where are you going?" he asked, staying Jill with a hand on her arm.

"To sit in back again so Erma can be up front."

"Don't." He ran his hand lightly up and down her arm. "Uh, Zoey will want to show Erma everything she bought."

She couldn't read his closed-off expression. Nevertheless she slid back in and shut her door. Mack's attitude toward her had changed on this trip. She couldn't begin to guess why. While it was infinitely nicer to stop sparring with him all the time, her self-respect was also threatened. From the moment she'd set eyes on him at the library, she'd known a part of her had never stopped loving him. She'd seen how easy it would be to fall under Mack's spell again so many times today. Luckily she only had to resist his potent appeal for a few more days. She could do that.

MACK WHEELED ERMA out, opened the back door and lifted her in.

"What did the doctor say?" J.J. asked, turning in her seat.

"Better news than I expected. I'm back to the original diagnosis of a bad sprain. What the doctor thought might be a hairline fracture was nothing. Still, it's four to six weeks off my feet. He wants me to taper off the pain meds, thank goodness."

"It's good Sonja can fill in," J.J. said. "I should probably book a hotel room for the rest of my stay so she can have my room at the ranch."

"I told Benny to put Sonja in an upstairs guest room." Mack's word on the subject brooked no further discussion.

"So, you had a good shopping trip?" Erma patted the pile of shopping bags on the seat between her and Zoey.

"Do you want to see what I bought? J.J. and Dad helped me."

"Your dad did? My, things are a-changin' at Turkey Creek Ranch. For the better." She poked J.J.'s shoulder through the headrest. "It's almost worth my taking a tumble. Listen, you guys didn't already eat lunch, did you? I worked up a powerful appetite with all that poking at my hip."

Mack chuckled. "We were hoping you'd be as hungry as we are. I know the perfect steak place. Hold on, we'll be there in a jiffy."

Chapter Ten

The next morning J.J. dressed for riding in jeans, boots and layers. She knew Texas weather on the high desert could change in a matter of minutes. The sturdy camera pack she used was ready, and stored in a borrowed backpack along with lip balm, sunscreen and a floppy hat that would work in sun or rain. Last night at supper when she mentioned preparing for rain, the men called her a greenhorn and laughingly reminded her that Texas was in the midst of a long drought.

She actually felt comfortable going off with Mack today. Sonja fit right in with the family and got along famously with Erma. Plus, Brandy was coming over to spend the day with Zoey and see her new things.

J.J. went to the kitchen, planning to make sandwiches for them to take along, and found Mack had beaten her to it. "Will a couple of roast beef sandwiches suit you? Sonja said you told her at breakfast that you weren't interested in tortillas and frijoles," he said with a teasing smile.

"I said I didn't want biscuits and beans," J.J. corrected him. "Do you have room in your saddlebags to toss in a couple of those apples?"

"Sure. What's in your bulging backpack?"

"Cameras, an extension tripod and other photography stuff."

"How many pictures do you plan to take?" he asked, storing the apples.

J.J. looked him over from head to toe. "I want a variety of photos our readers will love."

"Tell me again why city women who read your magazine give a rip about an ol' country boy like me?"

Hoisting her camera bag while Mack collected his water canteen and saddlebags, J.J. beat him to the door and shot back over her shoulder, "Are you joking? Women love ogling cowboys. We had a wide circulation, but our editor in chief said this monthly promo of hot, successful men has almost tripled our subscriptions. Women signed up in droves for a chance to win a night on the town with one of you single guys. Of course, they're probably hoping a night on the town might lead to something longer lasting." Her voice wobbled as she spoke.

"What?" Mack's tone caused her to stop abruptly. "What are you talking about?"

"Zoey told you the first day at the library. The magazine ran the pictures Zoey sent and readers emailed the magazine explaining why they'd like to meet you. It's the same for all of our featured men. We read the messages and run background checks on each potential winner to be sure she's not a kook or a stalker—or married," she said firmly. "A committee then chooses one woman per featured man who delivers a check for his charity on behalf of the magazine. Staff arrange a night out for the couple, which is filmed and photographed. Starry eyes, starry night, you know it'll be a big deal." She started toward the barn again.

"I completely missed that," he said. "So you'll be photographing my evening?"

"Probably not. *Her Own Woman* has several photographers. Our features editor gives us assignments, and so far the follow-ups haven't been handled by the initial photographer. I did shoot the evening out with Mr. January. Past months are archived on our website if you want to see them."

"So you won't come back? Can I request you?" he asked as Benny came out of the barn leading two saddled horses. One was a tall, spirited black gelding, the other a docile buckskin mare.

"Why would you request me?"

"I'm comfortable with you, and you know I'm a reluctant contestant."

He wanted her to come back? That gave J.J. pause as she blindly accepted the mare's reins from Benny. Hitching her pack higher on her back, she mounted the horse without much trouble. She stood so Benny could adjust her stirrups, and idly watched Mack secure his canteen and saddlebags and mount with enough grace to make her mouth go dry.

"Benny, I left Jiggs at the house. Jill noticed yesterday that he's limping. I can't see anything in his left front paw, but it's swollen and he didn't like me touching it. Have Delaney take a look. Jiggs may have picked up a mesquite thorn."

"Will do. You're getting a late start. You still planning to be back by supper?"

"Yep, since the guys said the herd settled down nicely. I sent Eldon to plow the south pasture. Trevor's going to town to pick up seed."

Benny touched the brim of his hat to acknowledge

Mack, who then led the way out of the barnyard. When he and Jill broke free of the charred grassland, Mack dropped back beside her. "So, will you come back?"

"Frankly, I thought you'd be delighted to see the last of me."

He hemmed and hawed, but finally said, "Well, Zoey would be in hog heaven if you came back and took her shopping again. Uh, me, too." Leaving it there, he kicked his horse into a trot.

It was a gait that slapped J.J.'s backpack so hard against her shoulder blades she worried for the safety of her expensive cameras. Hauling back on the mare, she looped the reins around her saddle horn and adjusted the buckles, tightening the pack's straps.

Mack circled his horse around and rejoined her. "Is everything all right?"

"Don't worry about me. As long as I can see you up ahead I won't get lost."

"If you plan to walk Ginger all the way there and home again, it'll be midnight before we complete our round trip."

J.J. patted the mare's neck. "Appropriate name. Hey, we could have started earlier."

"Not with all the phone calls I had to make this morning to the steak-fry committee. Most of them volunteer every year, but they're regular ranch folks busy with lots of other things. I had to make sure they're all available for our meeting tomorrow afternoon."

"Right. You said I could tag along. The meeting will round out my article nicely."

"I also said you should prepare to be bored." He smiled one of his heart-stopping smiles and J.J. decided she ought to speed up. The prospect of a night ride with Mack threatened to stir up too many old memories.

She indicated the barren land they were crossing. "Not even a scrub cedar in sight."

"After another hour or so you'll think we've entered a different country. Although the grass at the summer range isn't as lush this year as it usually is. I hope there's enough to fatten the calves and add the good kind of lean to my steers."

"You still love ranching, don't you?"

"Love it?" He shrugged. "Ranching is pretty much all I know. There's a certain thrill in the challenge, I suppose. But it's not as easy to make a profit like in Granddad's or even my dad's day. Some longtime ranchers in the area have packed it in because their kids weren't interested in carrying on. Developers snap up their land and the town steadily moves out, sucking up our limited water for golf courses. Those of us who are left have to ranch smarter."

"I hear that everywhere I travel. City dwellers multiply and urban sprawl gobbles up open land. It'd be a shame if that happened to Turkey Creek Ranch—it's a historic treasure. You'll have to encourage Zoey to fall in love with a young wannabe rancher, Mack."

"That'll be her choice. I've gotta say, though, she threw me into a panic when she followed me around with a camera and talked about taking photography classes next year. I imagined her being a nomad like you. I should've been relieved to discover her interest was all about entering me in a silly contest."

"You weren't happy that the contest brought me back into your life."

"You're putting words in my mouth, Jill. I'm not

keen on the contest, but I owe you a debt of gratitude for opening my eyes to how I've lost touch with Zoey."

J.J. thought about telling him that his daughter wanted a mother so badly she was willing to trust the magazine to vet a total stranger for the job. But she didn't know how to broach the subject without injecting her own opinions, so she turned back to ranching. "Is this all your land?"

"No, this is free range. Dad left me twenty-five thousand acres, but I sold some and now I'm at around twelve thousand, most used for soil conservation. It's taken me a long time and a lot of work and money to return native grasses to a third of my grazing land."

"The same native grasses that burned yesterday?"

"Don't remind me. At least when native grass burns, the roots don't die. Even before it sprouts back it slows erosion and continues to filter water going into underground aquifers. Providing we get a few good rainstorms. Do you really care about any of this?"

"Once I cared a lot, Mack," she said with honesty tinged by nostalgia.

He'd reined his horse in to ride abreast of J.J. They were so close his left leg bumped her right one and their mounts' noses brushed until his horse snuffled, shied and sidestepped away. Mack brought him back in line. "About this contest…I hate the idea of dating a stranger. I get that for whatever reason it's part of the package, but it's your magazine. So, come back in August and *you* be my date," he implored.

J.J.'s breath stalled for a moment. "It's not *my* magazine. I didn't make the rules, but they were printed on every entry form. A reader gets that honor, Mack."

"It's silly. God only knows why Zoey got it into

her head that I ought to date a stranger. You know she wants you to come back in the fall, Jill."

Their lower legs jostled against each other again, sending goose bumps up J.J.'s body. She waited for Mack to say he wanted her to come back, too. But he didn't. Disappointed, she edged her horse away from his to break their slight physical connection. "Sorry, but magazine personnel are barred from entering any of our contests. It's standard operating procedure."

His face fell, leaving J.J. to wonder if he'd been serious at all. Until he shrugged and said, "Well, do me a favor, then...send someone who looks like Heidi Klum."

"Talk about shallow."

He tipped back his head and laughed. He'd ridden close enough for J.J. to inhale his scent. That and the timbre of his laughter touched something deep inside her and left her a bit light-headed. It brought an aching reminder of how much she missed the way they used to tease each other. Those were some of her happiest memories.

Mack suddenly tacked to the right, altering their direction by about forty-five degrees.

J.J. noticed immediate changes in the countryside. There were more outcroppings of limestone, more gnarled shrubs, and while it wasn't pronounced, she sensed a rise in elevation. "There's something really beautiful about this desolate territory, Mack."

"Here I figured you'd be dying to get back to civilization by now."

"Not so much." She might have said more, but they rounded a copse of misshapen boulders and bent mesquite trees. Fanned out in a draw below, green grass met a blue sky streaked with peach-colored clouds. Grazing contentedly on both sides of a silver ribbon of river bisecting the draw was a sea of cattle. They all had curly, dark red coats and broad white faces. J.J. stopped, shrugged off her bag and dug out a camera. She attached her favorite long-range lens, propped her elbow on the saddle horn and began snapping away.

"Hey, I thought you wanted me in the pictures," Mack said.

"I will, but the colors are so vibrant now. As the sun sinks the panorama won't be the same. These shots are for me…to remember." She let her camera arm go lax. "Enough. Now we can ride down to the river and eat lunch. Then I'll decide where to pose you."

"Posed photos look…well, posed," he mumbled, starting his gelding on a slow descent toward the river.

"My job is to make them look natural," she called after him.

He dismounted on a low knoll a short distance from the river, next to a fire ring of rocks and signs of grass being matted down. "This okay? It's where we generally make camp when we bring in a herd."

"Any place is fine. I'm starved."

Mack checked his watch. "It's later than I thought. Going on three." He unhooked the canteen and passed it to J.J. "We need to head back in an hour. That'll put us at the ranch about when I told Benny to expect us."

Swinging down to the ground, J.J. instantly knew she'd been in the saddle too long for her first ride in quite a while.

Mack saw her rubbing her thighs. "Tenderfoot," he said, unpacking the apples and sandwiches.

She made a face at him and limped over. He spread

out a plaid blanket that had been rolled up behind his saddle. She dropped the canteen and the camera backpack, then eased down. "Oh, it feels heavenly to sit on terra firma," she said as Mack passed her a sandwich.

"You may not feel up to going with me to the steak-fry meeting tomorrow."

"I will. A dip in your hot tub after supper tonight will fix me up."

Mack pictured Jill in his hot tub as he ate his sandwich. She hadn't said it to make him want to join her later, but it did. He'd never expected to feel this way with any woman again.

Idly, Mack picked up an apple and polished it on his shirt, wondering if there was any chance in hell that they could start over.

Jill put her sandwich down and unzipped her bag. She swiftly changed lenses on her camera, rolled over onto her stomach and began taking pictures of Mack with the apple.

"Hey, what are you doing?"

"That's going to be a fantastic shot. Our readers will think you were about to tempt Eve with that apple."

He frowned at her in an attempt to erase what had really been on his mind. "Then I'll just go feed this apple to Zorro," he said, bounding to his feet.

"Who?" Jill wiggled around until she sat cross-legged, and traded her camera for her half-eaten sandwich.

"My horse," Mack said, heading to where both horses grazed.

"Here," Jill called. "Then give my apple to Ginger. It's only fair."

Mack came back reluctantly. He took the apple Jill held up, and when their fingers met he got all twisted up inside. With her hair tangled by the wind, her lips soft and pink, Mack was more than tempted to toss away the apples, tumble Jill onto the blanket and make love to her. Of course he wouldn't. He was far too civilized to give in to those urges. He took both apples and walked away.

J.J. finished her sandwich. "Stand right there between the horses," she instructed Mack. "Good, good." She circled around the animals, shooting them and Mack from several positions. "To get a wide-angle picture of you with the herd as a backdrop, I think it'll be better if I'm on Ginger and you walk down closer to the river. I want to feature you but also showcase what you do." Still sore from the ride, J.J. hobbled to Ginger. She had a hard time mounting while holding the camera. She could have asked Mack for help, but his attention was on the cows.

"Stop. The scenery with the river is perfect where you are." J.J. gathered the reins and nudged her horse downhill while continuing to focus Mack in the Nikon's viewfinder. All at once Ginger stumbled. The animal pitched forward and J.J. went flying over the buckskin's head. She landed shoulder-first in lumpy grass and rolled. For several seconds she couldn't catch her breath.

Mack bellowed and charged up the slope. Dropping to his knees he carefully slid his arms around her waist and turned her over. "Are you injured? My God, Jill, what happened?"

She spat out dirt and grass, shaking her head.

Mack gently dusted off her nose and eyebrows.

"Don't, that tickles," she managed to scold brokenly as she sucked in air. "I'm shaken, and I lost my breath. I think that's all. Go check on Ginger. She tripped and almost fell."

"This draw is riddled with prairie dog holes. If you're sure nothing's broken, I'll carry you to the blanket, and then have a look-see at Ginger."

J.J. nodded, and found herself lifted, whisked away and parked on the blanket. Little by little feeling returned to her chin. And it finally quit hurting to take a deep breath.

"Ginger didn't break anything," Mack announced from a few yards away, "but she's not bearing any weight on the left front leg." Rising, he unsaddled the mare and carried the gear to the blanket. "We're in a pickle. The mare needs transport back to the ranch where Delaney can treat her." Mack tugged his cell phone out of his pocket and frowned. He walked around and frowned harder. "I'm not getting any bars. Dang, but we need more cell towers."

"Zorro is okay. I'll stay here with Ginger, Mack. You ride to the ranch to get your pickup and a horse trailer."

"That could take up to five hours round trip. It's dark here once the sun sets. I mean dark as in pitch-black. I didn't plan to start a fire so I didn't bring matches. No, I won't leave you alone, Jilly. You landed harder than you're letting on." He knelt and touched her face lightly. "Benny will either come for us when we don't turn up, or he'll send Eldon or Trevor."

J.J.'s heart swelled. She covered his hand that lay against her cheek. "I'm so sorry, Mack. You won't have to put Ginger down, will you?" Tears trickled over their joined hands.

"No, no." Mack wiped her tears away. "It's probably a pulled tendon. The water in the river is cold this time of year. If I had something to wet and make a compress, it would keep the swelling to a minimum."

"I have a cloth in my camera pack that I use to clean lenses, and I use rubber bands to keep my filters in their bags. I wonder if we can secure a wet cloth around her leg."

"It's worth a try."

She started to get up to retrieve the pack.

"Stay," he said. "Rest."

"I'm fine, but if you insist."

He unzipped the camera backpack.

J.J. rubbed her arms. "I'm beginning to shake, but I tend to fall apart after a crisis is over."

Mack stripped off his jacket and draped it around her shoulders.

"Thanks." Pulling it close she took comfort from the warmth and from Mack's essence.

"Hey, you have a book of smushed matches. Oh, and some— Oh!" He was holding two condom packets.

"Yikes! Those were a joke from coworkers who thought they were being funny when I was assigned to take photos at Mardi Gras. Toss them. I didn't clean out my camera bag between assignments," she said, feeling a rush of embarrassment.

Mack arched one eyebrow, but put them back.

Worried about what he was thinking, J.J. watched him find the cloth, retrieve the rubber bands and hike to the river. When he returned, she couldn't take her

eyes off him——the play of muscles under his shirt as
he applied the compress and then made a fire with
dry wood and pine needles. He used most of her book
of matches to start the fledgling fire. Watching him
made her think about those condoms, and the very
notion swept aside what aches and pains she did have.

Stretching her hands out to the sputtering flame,
J.J. was surprised when Mack joined her on the blanket and wrapped her in his arms. "Your idea worked
like a charm," he murmured in her ear. "I'll change
Ginger's compress every so often until it gets too dark
to make my way to the river."

His low voice mesmerized her. She shivered, not
from cold this time, but from the texture of his five-
o'clock shadow.

"Aren't you warm yet? I worry that you may have a
concussion." Mack tilted up her face so he could look
deep into her eyes.

Her stomach cartwheeled at his closeness. "I don't
have a concussion," she insisted, turning to slip her
arms around his waist. "But I like the heat you're giving off." Rising up, she kissed him, something she'd
wanted to do since he'd left her that night on the patio.
If he pulled away now, she'd blame her indiscretion on
an addled brain, a result of her recent fall.

Caught off guard, Mack crushed her against his
chest. "Oh, Jilly. Oh, Jilly," he said in a breathless
whisper. He nipped her earlobe, then her neck, sliding
his hands beneath the jacket to peel it back. He had to
delve under two more layers of clothing to reach her
collarbone. Sighing, Mack traced his tongue along
the ridge until he got to the cleft between her breasts.
When her head fell languidly back, he ran his hands

up and down her sides and found her mouth again with his. Their kisses became more urgent, and he hurriedly began undressing her.

"You taste just as sweet as I remember," he said throatily.

J.J. slid her hands beneath his T-shirt, her fingers coming to rest on his chest. It felt like a furnace and his heart jumped erratically. She felt her own pulse ratchet up. "What are we doing, Mack?" She grew still, waiting for an answer.

"Catching up," he responded in a rasp that had her seeking the fly of his jeans. He helped by kicking off his boots, then worked fast to get rid of the rest of the clothing that kept her breasts from his sight, from his roaming mouth. "Scoot that bag over here, darlin'. Remind me to send your coworkers a big thank-you. Oh, wait… Are you really okay?"

"Never better," she insisted, and surged against him as she heard him rip open a pack. After he sheathed himself, she wanted to kiss him again. But she managed to say, "Mack, we haven't talked about the past."

"Forget the past," he said, stripping away the last of her clothing. "We'll start over with a clean slate." He barely managed to say because his muscles tensed when their bodies meshed, causing J.J. to moan in pleasure. His words burned into her brain and then she simply gave up thinking about anything at all except how right it all felt, having her mouth, her breasts, her belly pressed under the weight of Mack's long, lean body. She was back where she belonged and everything was right with her world. She wrapped her legs around him, pulling him deeper in spite of twinges of saddle soreness.

Afterward, after she'd caught her breath for the second time that day, J.J. liked that neither of them rushed to untangle their limbs.

"I want you in my life. Forever," Mack whispered, smiling even more than usual. She played with his dark hair, stained reddish in the molten glow of the sunset. All she managed was a nod in the middle of a big yawn. Mack chuckled and leaned in to run his tongue across her lips one last time. "Before we both fall asleep, we should get dressed. Much as I hate to move, I need to wet Ginger's bandage again before I can't see my hand in front of my face."

She stretched, but sat up. "You're right. It wouldn't do for Benny or your wranglers to find us like this."

"I doubt we'll see hide nor hair of anyone before nine. Cold as it gets on the high plains, we may wish someone would show up sooner."

Never, she told herself, watching him get dressed and pull on his boots before collecting Ginger's towel. If she had her druthers right now, she'd stay here forever.

He refreshed Ginger's leg poultice, sat down beside her again and kissed her. "I think the compress is helping."

"I'm glad. But I feel so bad that I didn't see the hole."

Mack placed another kiss on her mouth. Then he broke apart a rotten piece of cedar and set the pieces on the struggling fire. Unfortunately, the meager blaze didn't throw out a lot of heat. But the dancing flames and the weight of Mack's arm around her soon let J.J. fall asleep.

He stayed awake marveling at how easy and wonderful it was to renew their romance. Deep inside, he'd always known his hunger for Jill had never abated.

BENNY, ACCOMPANIED BY Jiggs, rumbled up in Mack's pickup around nine-thirty. Mack gently laid Jill down, pillowing her head, which had been resting against his cramped shoulder, on her saddle. He tucked half the blanket around her and walked over to greet the man emerging from the pickup. Mack slapped Benny's back. "You're a welcome sight. How the heck did you know to bring a horse trailer? I figured I'd have to leave you here with Ginger and make another round trip to the ranch to bring back a trailer. She got her hoof stuck in a hole and took a stumble."

"I asked myself what would happen to keep you out with a bunch of steers well after sundown," Benny said. "The only thing that made sense was that one of the horses had gone lame. Is Jill okay? Or should I have driven slower to get here?" Mack's old friend said slyly.

Thankfully, Jiggs interrupted by scrambling into the front seat of the pickup, whining and holding up a bandaged paw. Mack ruffled the dog's fur. "Could Delaney figure out how he injured himself?" he asked, inspecting the bandage that ran halfway up the collie's leg.

"Somehow he drove a sliver of limestone between two toes. It was in so deep Delaney had to anesthetize him to remove it. You're avoiding my question about Jill, boss."

"When Ginger stepped in a hole, Jill sailed over her head and did a face plant. She wasn't badly hurt, and it turned out good. Better than good, Benny. We patched things up and I've never been happier."

"Hot dang. There'll be call to celebrate once we get y'all home."

Mack glanced over. The woman beside the dying fire had begun to stir. "Uh, let's keep this between us for now. Jill's job is still in New York. We didn't discuss how we might make things work. I'd prefer Zoey not fly over the moon with excitement until Jill and I come to definite terms."

The older man lightly punched Mack's arm. "Gotcha! My lips are sealed until you make it official."

Chapter Eleven

Sonja wheeled Erma to the breakfast table. "Where's Jill?" Erma directed her question at Mack, who'd dished up a breakfast burrito from a steaming stack Benny's jolly cousin set on the table. "I hope Jill's not suffering from her fall."

"She's sleeping in." Mack accepted the salsa from Eldon and spooned some over his burrito. "She wouldn't come in from the barn last night until the vet examined Ginger. That ran extra late because the vet filling in for Delaney had to drive here from his clinic in Seminole."

Benny gestured at the others with his fork. "Apparently Delaney's son had to be admitted to the Lubbock hospital for tests. Nickolas is running unexplained fevers again."

Erma frowned. "Do the doctors here think Nick's leukemia is back?"

"Maybe." Mack looked grim. "I didn't tell Zoey when I went up to say good-night. I'd appreciate if you all keep that under your hats until they're sure."

"Zoey's got other things on her mind. Today she and Jill plan to print the photos Jill took," Erma said.

Mack set down his burrito and stood. "I'll go see

if Zoey and Jill arranged a specific time. After the vet left last night Jill uploaded the pictures she took of me. She fiddled with them on my office computer until close to 2:00 a.m. Then she got lucky with our spotty internet service and she was able to email them to her assistant in New York. But she's going with me to the steak-fry lunch meeting. I don't know if Jill remembered to tell Zoey."

Before he had a chance to leave, Zoey barreled into the kitchen, nearly bowling Mack over. "Whoa, whoa." He stopped her forward momentum. He held her still as Jiggs limped past them to get to his food bowl. "Now, what's got you up before the rooster crows?" Mack asked.

Zoey laughed. "The rooster already crowed bunches of times. I'm up because Brandy called. Her mom will pay us to pick strawberries and green beans today. Mrs. Evers has to arrange flowers for Raedean Foley's wedding. Is that okay? Her mom'll bring me home after she delivers the flowers to the church."

"Sure," Mack said. "I guess you and Jill can print your photographs later."

"Oh, yeah, I forgot. Is J.J. still asleep?" Zoey scanned the breakfast table.

"Yep. She hasn't surfaced yet."

"Maybe she won't need me. She'll know which ones are best. But I don't want you to see them, Daddy."

"Why not?"

Zoey made a face. "It's a surprise."

"Uh-huh. So does your all-fired hurry to go to the Everses' to earn money have to do with the same surprise?"

She stammered. "N-no. I th-thought if I earned the

money you'd let me get my ears pierced when Brandy does hers."

Mack made a sort of choking sound.

Benny, Eldon and Trevor left the table and carried their plates to the sink. "Whooee, chores are calling us, boss," Benny said as the men donned their hats and hustled toward the back door. Jiggs even flopped down on his belly, covering his nose with his paws as if awaiting some fallout.

"Come eat, you two," Erma called to Mack and Zoey. "And don't be squabbling or Sonja will change her mind about sticking around."

The other woman chuckled. "Actually, it brings back memories of some lively discussions my husband, rest his soul, had with our daughters over multiple ear piercings and tasteful tattoos—and I use the term *tasteful* loosely."

"We will not even speak of tattoos," Mack said, sitting down again.

Zoey giggled and kissed his cheek before she slid into her chair. "One little hole in each ear is all I want."

Mack added more salsa to his cooling burrito. He thought about Jill's earrings. Her jewelry was always classy. That day at the library, Zoey had cried about the kids at school who said she looked like a cowboy, not a girl. Mack didn't want that. "Tell you what, Bug. You earn half of what you need and I'll pay the other half."

"Really?" She flew out of her chair and hugged his neck tight. "Oh, boy, oh, boy, wait till I tell Brandy. Daddy, I love you, even if you call me Bug. Can we go now so I can start picking berries?"

He pried her arms loose, aware that Erma and Sonja were amused. "Grab a burrito and then go get what you need for the day. And thank Jill when you see her," he said, sounding gruffer than necessary. "Jill wears earrings and they look…okay."

Zoey plucked up a burrito and flew from the room. He was sure that Erma and Sonja saw through him. Without another word he snatched another burrito, jammed on his hat and headed out to his pickup to wait for Zoey.

JILL WAS UP by the time he got back, looking fresh as a sunflower. She was wearing earrings with blue stones that looked like a cloudless sky. She sat on the patio, her milky coffee on the table. No one else was around, and Mack approached her with purpose in his stride. Lifting her out of her chair, he kissed her thoroughly, tasting the sugar she always used in her coffee.

She gave in after her initial surprise and knocked his hat off as she buried her fingers in his hair, kissing him back with fervor.

Mack was slow to release her lips and set her on her feet again.

"Wow, cowboy," she teased, sliding her hands slowly down his chest. "To what do I owe that greeting?"

"Earrings," he said, then explained his conversation with Zoey as he swept up his hat.

"I'm glad you agreed to let her get her ears pierced, Mack. It'll mean she's not the odd girl out at school next year."

"It took a while, but I finally got that, Jill. If you don't mind going to town early, could you help me pick out a pair? I want to surprise her."

"Sure. Just let me grab my purse and we can go. How are all the infirm today?"

"Huh?"

"Erma, Ginger and Jiggs."

"Erma's feisty as ever. Jiggs isn't limping as much. And when Benny and I checked Ginger at dawn, the swelling in her leg was down and she ate all her oats."

"That's a relief. Okay. Do you want to take your truck? Or we can use my rental if we don't really need the pickup for anything today."

He dangled his keys. "If you're going to be a ranch wife, you'll have to get comfortable using a pickup for everything."

Jill skidded to a stop at the edge of the patio. "Ranch wife?" she squeaked.

Mack froze, puzzled. "What did you think last night was all about? What did it mean to you? I was serious when I said we've already wasted too much time. I want you in my life permanently. Don't you want the same?"

"Uh… I do. I just… Well, it all happened so fast."

"I don't call a thirteen-year gap fast."

"You have a point," she said slowly. They'd stopped at her room so she could collect her purse and note-book.

"Jill, what I'm trying to say is, will you be my wife?"

She couldn't identify why she felt troubled. She was finally exactly where she'd always wanted to be—with Mack at Turkey Creek Ranch. *But…and there was a but.* Before she could voice her concerns—over the speed with which this came about, and thoughts about the old indiscretion with Faith that he wasn't willing to discuss—she found herself saying, "Yes."

Thirty minutes later, after celebratory kisses, they stopped at the only jewelry store in town, where they selected a pair of gold stud earrings for Zoey. J.J. asked to have Mack's purchase put in a black velvet jewelry bag. He had leaned toward buying Zoey her birthstone, but JJ said, "Come back and buy the topaz earrings in November for her birthday. Gold is best for new piercings."

Before leaving the store, Mack lingered over a case of wedding sets. "Is there a ring you like here? I still have your engagement ring, but I can afford a bigger diamond now, Jilly."

Caught off guard, she tugged him toward the door. "Let's not discuss rings yet, Mack. I still live and work in New York."

"How much time do you need to quit and get back here?"

She stumbled. "Uh...a two weeks' notice at least. But, Mack, we have a lot of stuff to work out. You have your steak-fry in July, and your contest win has to play out, per your contract with the magazine. That's August 20th."

Mack grumbled something indecipherable as he opened the door to the restaurant where he had booked a back room for the luncheon meeting.

They entered the back room where the committee was to meet and Mack was instantly mobbed. Mostly, J.J. noticed, by women. She tried to step away, but he tightened his hold on her waist, effectively molding her to his hip. A sultry, dark-haired woman in a tight red sheath dress nonetheless attached herself to his left arm. Talk swirled around him. Some of the people asked Mack about the fire, some about Erma's health. Others chatted about the steak-fry.

A woman with graying hair, whom J.J. didn't recognize, wanted to know if Mack had heard that Delaney Blair's son was in the hospital again, and that she needed monetary help. "I think we should start a fund at the bank to help her," the woman said.

"I'll kick it off with a thousand," Mack immediately said. The woman typed a note in her smartphone, then left to corral someone else.

The persistent woman in the red dress clung to Mack tenaciously. "Mackenzie, is this your new housekeeper?" she cooed. "Amanda Evers said Benny's cousin came to fill in for Erma."

Mack pulled away. "This is my fian—"

J.J. leaned forward, cutting Mack off. "Nice to meet you," she said. "I'm J. J. Walker, a houseguest at Mack's ranch."

Some people seemed to have heard she was a magazine photographer from New York and began plying her with questions.

"Hey," Mack said, raising his voice. "We're supposed to be here to gear up for the steak-fry. Trudy, everyone, take your seats. Committee chairs can start giving reports while Buddy and his staff serve our food."

The room quieted. Mack pulled out a chair for J.J. and sat beside her, leaving Trudy Thorne to alternately pout and glare at them.

Mack took a notepad out of his shirt pocket and called on his first chairperson.

"Ticket sales are going well," a silver-haired matronly woman seated behind Trudy said. "We're already up by ten percent over this time last year. Your decision to advertise in neighboring towns has bolstered program ad sales. This being our fourth year, it's all running smoothly."

Two waitresses served iced tea and sandwiches. Reports continued and Mack jotted notes. "This is good," he praised everyone after the last chairwoman spoke. "We've got this down to a science. Moving our event to Labor Day weekend is a great idea, Freda." Mack smiled at a woman in big glasses. "I'm impressed with the entertainment you've booked. I think we can skip meeting again until after the Fourth of July. Call me if you hit any snags."

No one objected so Mack adjourned the meeting. He and J.J. went straight to the cashier, where he got the bill for all of the food. Trudy barged in as he handed over his debit card.

"Mack, what's your rush?" She muscled her way between him and J.J. As soon as he had his card back and had signed the receipt, he reached right around her, clasped J.J.'s wrist and led her out the door.

"Wait," Trudy called, following him down the sidewalk. "I want to invite you to go with me to the Fourth of July rodeo dance. I'll call you next week to get it on your calendar."

"Trudy, I don't…" But she was already crossing the street. Mack grimaced and climbed into the pickup.

"Is she someone you've been dating?" J.J. broke the dead silence.

"No. Never. Since her last divorce she's been hitting on me."

"I can see that."

"If you're jealous there's no need to be."

"I'm not." J.J. punched his arm. "I just know Zoey's not fond of her."

"Me, neither. She doesn't seem to get the message. And there are folks in town who've tried to set us up. Folks who think every single person should be part of a couple."

"I'd forgotten that about really small towns. It's so much harder to find someone in a city."

"You never did?"

"No." J.J. shook her head. "I think my heart always belonged to you, Mack," she said lightly, then changed the subject. "Is Zoey going to be home when we get there? I promised to print the pictures I took of her."

"She said for you to go ahead. She's picking strawberries with Brandy to earn some money for half the cost of her earrings. Out of curiosity why doesn't she want me to see the pictures? They aren't way out, are they?"

"No," she laughed. "But if I told you it would ruin her surprise."

"Okay, but remember, the printer is in *my* bedroom."

"You still can't peek. Don't you have things to do around the ranch?"

"Of course. But it'll be more fun to watch you fuss with your photos."

He slowed at the turn onto his ranch road, leaned over and kissed her. "I could get used to this."

"Me, too." She tasted his kiss on her lips and thought she really *could* get used to this togetherness. At one time, they'd been totally compatible, and trust was slowly returning. Finally she was beginning to believe they could make being together work. Turning her head, she smiled as she watched his hands on the steering wheel. She loved looking at them and loved feeling them caress her skin. A shiver went up her backbone.

"What are you thinking?" he asked.

"Something X-rated," she said.

His eyes widened. He slammed on the brakes in front of the house, stopping in a cloud of dust. Letting the motor idle he took Jill's upper arms and pulled her partway across the console and first nipped her lower lip, then kissed it better. "Want to go inside and tumble across my bed?"

"Um, that sounds promising." She ran a finger over his damp lips. "Can you hang on to that thought until later? I really want to crop and print Zoey's photos."

Mack pretended to give her option serious thought before he nodded, set her back in her seat and pulled the key from the ignition. "I'll try to behave while I watch you work."

"You can be in the room with me, but you can't peek at the pictures, okay? I gave Zoey my word."

"Fine. Shall I get us a lemonade?"

"Good idea. We both need to cool off. I'll drop my purse in my room, collect the photo paper and meet you in your *office*." She laid heavy accent on that word.

He hurried around the cab and opened her door. They parted with a lingering touch of the barest of fingertips.

From her room, she crossed the patio, entering Mack's bedroom from the poolside. She beat him there. In the alcove that doubled as his office, she booted up her laptop, accessed her photography software and turned on Mack's printer. Waiting for him to arrive, she wandered around his bedroom, studying things she'd not taken time to observe before. Other than the crocheted bedspread hanging again on the quilt rack, the room was wholly masculine with dark walls and dark wood furniture. Two eight-by-ten glossy photographs hung on the wall behind his nightstand. On taking a closer look, J.J. saw they were two of her early photographs. The sunset at South Padre Island brought back warm memories, as did the print below, which she recalled taking of their group of college friends their senior year. Everyone was so young and happy then, she thought, studying each face. She wondered why none of them had kept in touch.

Mack came in carrying two glasses of lemonade. Bending, he kissed the back of her neck before handing her one of the glasses. "I can give you nicer photos to hang on your wall. All centered better. I took these so early in my career I'm ashamed of how rough they are."

"I like them, so hands off," he said, flopping down on his bed.

Smiling, J.J. carried her drink to the alcove. "No peeking over my shoulder, now," she reminded him, and soon immersed herself in work. "Zoey is so photogenic," she said, half to herself. "It's not easy choosing between these shots." She printed the one of Zoey and her horse and slipped it into a folder to keep Mack from seeing it. She passed over the next two, but chose the following one, a photo of Zoey in the gold jacket, head slightly tilted, laughing as sun flooded the patio. Her hair appeared redder, her hazel eyes greener, and

her mouth uptilted on one side. J.J. blinked as she was
starkly reminded of someone else—a face she'd just
viewed in the group photo hanging on Mack's wall.
But not Faith's. Her stomach tensed. Forcing her legs
to support her, J.J. got up, snatched the picture off
the wall and sat heavily beside Mack on the bed. She
grabbed his hand.

He bolted up off the pillow. "Are you okay? You
look like you've seen a ghost."

"I have," she said, licking her lips. "Mack, I don't
know a delicate way to put this, but I have to ask.
What if…what if Zoey's not your daughter?" she
blurted.

Mack stiffened.

"I'm sorry. I hate to speak ill of the dead, but I
took a picture of Zoey that's a younger version of
Tom Corbin." She drew Mack's attention to a laughing man in the college print. "During Zoey's and my
photo shoot I had an odd sense of déjà vu when I was
centering her in my viewfinder. It's blatantly obvious
now, why. God, I'm so sorry, but look for yourself!"

Mack clapped his hand over her mouth. "Shh. No
one knows. Not Erma, not Benny, not Tom's family, or Faith's. I promised her I'd keep her secret. She
seemed to know I'd have to fight her folks in court to
keep them from raising Zoey. See, their religion is a
cult. Faith grew up under fear and abuse. Her parents
did try to take Zoey. The land I told you I sold… The
money went to pay legal fees. No matter what," he
said fiercely, "Zoey is *my* daughter." He thumped his
chest. "I walked the floor with her many nights. I
tended her boo-boos. I took her to her first day of kin-
dergarten. My name's on her birth certificate."

J.J. blanched. "I don't understand. I heard Faith crying, telling you she was pregnant, and you said you'd handle everything. I...I... You acted like you'd gotten her pregnant."

"What are you talking about?"

"The night I left! I came by to tell you about the scholarship to the Sorbonne. I wanted us to move up our wedding date and then I wouldn't go to Paris. I saw you and Faith in the kitchen. I...heard...it all. It hurt me so much, I ran away."

Mack gripped her arms. "I loved you. I thought you loved me. How could you think I'd sleep with anyone else? All this time..." His eyes blazed and he squeezed her arms. "You believed so ill of me?"

"Stop, you're hurting me, Mack."

He released her at once, but she stood, dropped the college photo on his bed and rubbed her arms. "I did love you, Mack. How could I stay after what I overheard? You never tried to get in touch after I sent back your ring."

"I had no idea why you sent it back. I was frantic. I called your mom. She said you had a better opportunity and took it. She said you left because your main goal was to advance your career."

"Yes, well, we both know my mother glories in status. But, Mack, you have to tell Zoey the truth. She's old enough to understand. Tom has parents and a sister who deserve to know. Zoey may have cousins near her age. No good can come from hiding the truth."

Mack sliced a hand through the air. "Telling her is out of the question. Reverend Adams would reopen their custody suit. Faith and Tom had planned to elope. When he was killed she was scared to death to tell her folks she was pregnant. I volunteered to let her stay here until she could decide what to do. And then you took off, so don't lecture me, okay? Anyway, what makes a parent if not love?"

"Trust! How can you ask me that? You saw me fall apart when I found out my mother let me live a lie. No matter the kind of man my real dad was, she stole my choice to meet him. Is that what you want for Zoey?"

"Not an issue. She's never going to find out about Tom. If you'd stuck around, Faith would have let us adopt her baby. That's what she hoped—that you and I would take her baby, rather than let her be raised in a cult. She didn't have the strength to fight her folks alone. They'd always intimidated her."

"I'm sorry, Mack. I knew Faith had a difficult home life. But…compounding wrongs doesn't make a right."

"It's for me to decide, Jill. You left me. I protected Faith the only way I could. Her doctors said she was risking her life to have Tom's baby. When she went into premature labor, I swore to keep her secret. It's my name on Zoey's birth certificate. I *am* her father. If you can't accept that, then you and I have no chance, Jill."

Pain ripped through her. She saw that Mack meant what he said. The love she thought they'd rekindled snuffed out like a candle. It was all she could do to walk back to the printer and print the telltale photo of Zoey. She added it to the folder. "Give these to Zoey, please," she said, her voice unsteady. "I'll pack and be gone from here before Amanda Evers brings Zoey home." Head held high, she left Mack. In the tile hallway her boot heels clicked ominously. Every step rang out, *Finished, finished, finished.*

She packed swiftly. Her heart hurt too badly for her to find Erma to say goodbye. J.J. wrote her a note that simply said something had come up in New York. She addressed it to Erma, but left it on her pillow. J.J. had never expected to fall in love with Mack again, but she had, and the pain of leaving this second time threatened to be even worse than the first. She didn't want to cry on the drive back to Lubbock, but she did.

Chapter Twelve

Because she'd switched her plane ticket, J.J. had to make several stops and arrived at her apartment mid-morning a day after she left Texas. The only positive thing about the long trip was that it gave her ample opportunity to write and send in the article on Mack. It was a load off her mind. And yet, in the aftermath of the joyous camaraderie at the ranch, her home felt empty—like her heart.

Off and on she checked her cell phone, hoping Mack would call to say he had thought things over and saw her point about not letting Zoey live a lie. Mack had his family history that made him proud. Tom Corbin probably had a proud family history, too. And yet, there were no missed calls on her phone.

Exhausted as she was, she couldn't stand the silence, but neither did she feel like getting together with friends. She settled on going to Sunday brunch at a favorite café, hoping to reacclimate to her life—to city life. She ate a calorie-laden cinnamon roll while fashioning a mental list of everything she already missed about Texas—the ranch, yes. Zoey, Benny, Erma and Sonja, but above all, Mack. *This was not helping her.*

She paid her bill and went to a movie, a sad one where no one cared if she cried. Walking home afterward, J.J. decided she'd wallowed in self-pity long enough. She unpacked and prepared to go to work on Monday. She had laundry to keep her occupied until then. Laundry and nagging thoughts that she might have been too hasty, too harsh in her judgment. She'd done that once and had been terribly wrong. She'd misjudged Mack and Faith.

Poor Faith. J.J. dug clothes out of the dryer and imagined what she might have done in Faith's place. While her own mom had been difficult at times, J.J. had never been browbeaten, or worse, abused.

And Mack, heavens, he had really done an honorable thing, marrying a woman he knew to be in trouble and in ill health—when there was every reason to believe he would be left to raise a baby alone. Anybody with eyes could see he adored Zoey as if she were his own. He and Erma had given Zoey love and solid values.

JJ looked around. Her clothes were done and now what? She still had too many hours to wrestle with her conscience.

AT TURKEY CREEK Ranch, Mack acted like a grouchy bear. He didn't join the family for supper the evening Jill left. During breakfast the next day he ignored questions about her precipitous departure.

"I need to call J.J., Dad, and thank her for printing my pictures. I didn't think she'd leave before we had a chance to say goodbye. I have to email her."

"You don't," Mack said, glowering at everyone who

watched him with interest. Zoey's lips quivered as she fought unhappiness.

Mack poured ketchup on his scrambled eggs instead of salsa, something he never did. "Zoey, just forget that Jill Walker came here and disrupted our lives."

She stared openmouthed at her dad. Benny, too, reared his head. "What happened to you and Jilly patching things—"

Mack cut Benny off with a dark scowl. He abruptly bolted up, grabbed his hat off the rack and stomped out the back door, leaving everyone in the room staring from his blood-red eggs to the still-vibrating screen door.

"Eat up, y'all," Erma gestured with her fork. "Can't let good food go to waste all because Mackenzie's ham-headed."

J.J.'s BOSS POKED her head around the corner of the break room where J.J. stood alone, doctoring her coffee. "Here you are," Donna said. "The article and photos you sent in for our hot August cowboy are sensational. We replaced the original pictures on our website with your new ones. We'd already received dozens of entries. Everyone wants to be the lucky lady to deliver the check for that hottie's charity."

J.J. poured yet another heaping spoonful of sugar into her already sweet coffee. "Donna, I'd like to help pick the winner."

Donna leaned against the counter. "Why? Up to now you've avoided that chore like the plague."

Selfish reasons cycled through J.J.'s head, but she only said, "Mack's daughter is so sweet. And as you know, she wants a mom, a woman her dad can fall instantly in love wi-with." J.J. stumbled over her last word.

Donna stared at J.J. "Why don't I think you'll find anyone suitable?"

J.J. had to turn away from her boss's all-seeing gaze. "Please. At least let me double-check the background reports."

"Okay. Frankly I had no idea about the popularity of cowboys. I'm considering extending the campaign for another year and doing twelve months of nothing but cowboys and ranchers."

Donna's secretary buzzed the room to say she had a phone call, so she ducked out.

J.J. followed, going to her own cubicle to do nothing but stare at the wall. Next year didn't matter. She told herself Mack would be old news by then. He could well be old-married-news by then.

For the most part, the rest of her week was crappy. She felt confined and depressed. June 1st, Mack's birthday, passed. JJ found herself wanting to call Zoey to see what her dad thought of the birthday photographs. But she resisted.

June dragged on. JJ gagged on every contest entry Donna sent over for her to read. She grew restless and yet she didn't ask for an international assignment even though New York's streets felt too crowded, her apartment, hollow. Friends invited her to a Fourth of July party, but she declined. Moping about at home, she wondered if Mack had capitulated and gone to the holiday dance with Trudy Thorne. Her jealousy flared as red as the dress she remembered the brazen woman wearing.

Knowing this wasn't good for her, she went shopping on the weekend. She only bought items for Zoey. A cute gray wool jacket, natural makeup designed for teens, a polka-dot cardigan and shampoo with an orange scent. Lastly, a book on braid styles—since the ranch had sporadic internet access at best, JJ thought the book would come in handy if Zoey wanted to try some new looks. She carefully packed everything and shipped the box before talking herself out of it. Mack wouldn't like her resurfacing in his life—or Zoey's. Actually, a hope lingered that he might be so angry with her that he'd phone. And wasn't that pathetic— her wanting to hear his voice at any cost? So many times she'd started to call him. But darn-it-all, she wanted him to make the first move.

She capitulated to Donna's request that she go to London and shoot winter fashions. It should have taken her mind off Mack, but didn't. Before leaving New York, she reviewed the finalists to win the date with Mack. All of the women had been background-checked and approved. Donna had been right—J.J. found fatal flaws in all of the women.

While she was in London, J.J.'s mom phoned, sounding young and excited, announcing her plans to marry Arne Biddle. J.J. no longer needed to subsidize her mother's apartment. Mercy, that meant she could finally think about leaving her day job. It should have made her ecstatic but only underscored the fact that her mom was on husband number three while J.J. had spent years loving one man who didn't love her enough in return. *Oh, but was that fair?*

Home August 1st, J.J. wearily unpacked and tried to figure out if she could afford to quit *Her Own Woman* in order to freelance. She was so deep in thought that her cell phone startled her when it rang. Her heart seized as she recognized the La Mesa prefix. "He…llo," she managed, in spite of barely breathing.

"Jill? It's Erma."

J.J.'s heart plunged. "Erma, are you all right? Is something wrong at the ranch?"

The housekeeper tsked. "I'm up and walking. Not running any footraces yet. Sonja's leaving us next week."

"That's…nice," J.J. said.

"I just wanted to see how you're doing. Zoey got your gifts and you're all she can talk about. Not about the gifts, but about how much she misses you."

"Um, I'm glad she likes what I sent."

"Well, the more she mentions you, the more sullen Mack is. Mind if I ask what went on between you two? Benny and I want to know if either of us can help heal the rift, whatever happened."

"Oh, Erma." J.J. started to cry, finally allowing herself to explain what happened the night she'd come across Mack consoling the newly pregnant Faith. She didn't mention the cause of their last argument.

Erma listened without interruption until J.J. wound down, then she said, "Jill, Mack's marriage was never right. I saw that. Faith's bad heart was a result of rheumatic fever not treated when she was young. She knew pregnancy was a risk. One day when I drove her to the *doctor, she flat out told me she loved another man*—a college friend of Mack's who was killed in a motorcycle wreck. Guy by the name of Tom. Faith said she'd do anything to keep Reverend Adams from getting his hooks in her baby. I shouldn't share this, but…Faith didn't sleep in Mack's room. And yet, after she passed, he had her buried in the Bannerman family plot."

"That's a good thing for Zoey," J.J put in.

"Right, but it incensed Faith's daddy. Mack shelled out a fortune to keep custody of Zoey. Faith's folks sued to raise her, but the judge ruled for Mack." At J.J.'s silence, Erma added, "I probably should've kept all of that to myself, but something I know is families don't have to be blood. Zoey, me, Benny, Mack, we'd all be in hog heaven if you'd come back. You love him, don't you?"

J.J. sighed. "I can't deny it. I always have. But sometimes love isn't enough, Erma."

"Of course it is. Love trumps everything that happens in life. Anyway, I've gotta go. Suppertime. Come back, please. If you can't, at least call Zoey."

Throughout the night J.J. wrestled with her addled brain and her weighty heart. In the morning she was bleary eyed as she watched a smoldering August sun try to cut through Manhattan's haze. She'd come to several realizations. First, she knew now that her love for Mack was strong. Second, despite how heartbroken she'd been over her mother and Rex's deception, she forgave them. They only did what they thought was best for her. Wasn't that where Mack stood? In his eyes Zoey was *his* child. And truthfully, Zoey might be happier to not have to deal with the truth until she was grown up.

J.J. showered, dressed and took a cab to work. They'd hit the wire to pick the reader to send to meet Mack on August 20th.

At noon, J.J. walked into Donna's office and shut the door. "I have a confession and a request," she said without preamble. "I've loved Mackenzie Bannerman since we were in college. I broke up with him and we went our separate ways due to a stupid misunderstanding. But I never stopped loving him. You sent me back there and I've walked away from him again. I've been miserable ever since."

Donna rolled a pen between her hands. "I've seen that, J.J. We all have. You're a fine photographer. I'd hate to lose you. I have to choose a reader today to go meet him. Plane tickets and other arrangements need to be settled. What can I do to help you?"

"I can't resolve things with Mack from here. I want you to send me with his check. I believe I'm the only reader who can fulfill Zoey Bannerman's wish for a mother." J.J. handed her boss a letter she'd composed that morning, her entry to the contest. It made Donna a bit weepy.

"I'm fully aware that I can't work for the magazine and be considered," J.J. said. "For a long time I've dreamed of freelancing. So I'm also tendering my resignation." She set a shorter note on top of the tearstained letter.

Donna cleared her throat. "This is actually a timely request, J.J. As much as I hate to, I need to cut some corners for the budget, and I'd save a fair amount on the benefits package if you and Joaquin went freelance." Standing, Donna offered her hand. "Consider both of your requests done. I wish you luck with freelancing. Keep in touch. I'll still send work your way," she said, ushering J.J. to the door where they stopped and hugged.

"Go see Pam in HR. She'll have the packet you

need as our August winner," Donna finished, smiling
as she stepped back into her office and shut the door.

THAT AFTERNOON J.J. boarded a flight to Texas. The
butterflies that began in her stomach when the plane
lifted off after a brief stopover in Dallas flapped
harder once she'd landed in Lubbock. They grew
worse after she rented a vehicle and drove toward
La Mesa. Time dragged. She dallied, driving far too
slowly.

Still, the minute she turned onto Mack's private
road she slowed the car to a veritable crawl. Afraid she
might be physically ill, J.J. parked behind his pickup
and sat, trying to settle her nerves. It startled her to
see Mack and Zoey emerge from the house, each pulling a suitcase.

*They were going on a trip. She should have called
before coming.* But she assumed he'd be here for the
magazine's event. Maybe he'd called it off. Heaven
knew he'd never welcomed the whole notion.

Expecting to be rebuffed, J.J. decided to tell Mack
she'd come solely to deliver the magazine's check for
his charity and save him from going out with a perfect stranger. She put on a brave face, got out of the
car and hesitated.

Zoey saw her first. She dropped the handle of her
bag and launched herself at J.J. "You're here. You're
really here! Daddy and me were going to go see you in
New York." Zoey practically squeezed the breath out
of J.J. even as her gaze lit on Mack for confirmation.

He bent and righted Zoey's suitcase, but J.J. saw his
expression burgeon with hope. "I should have given
you a call," he said. "We could have passed each other
on the highway. Why are you here, Jill?"

"Uh, I...brought the check from the magazine for your charity. I'm, uh, we're supposed to go out on the town when I present it...so...I can take follow-up photos for the magazine. Why were you going to New York?" she asked belatedly.

Mack nudged Zoey aside and he rested his hands on J.J.'s waist. "I told Zoey...about Tom," he said with feeling. "I fought with you over something I've always known I needed to face. You were right to leave. But...the truth is...I don't want to live without you."

J.J. clutched his shirtfront, too overwhelmed to speak.

Zoey hovered, anxiously biting her lip. "The same goes for me."

Glancing at Zoey, J.J. saw that she wore her hair in a neat French braid, and had on the cute polka-dot cardigan J.J. had sent her. The little girl she'd been in May was gone, and in her place—a young woman. J.J. reached out and touched Zoey's cheek.

"It's okay, J.J. Dad explained a lot of stuff about him and my mom. He showed me a picture you took in college. Tom Corbin looks nice. I should be sad he's dead, but I never met him. I said it'll be okay to meet his mom and dad if they want, but my home is here," she added fiercely.

"Definitely," J.J. agreed. "I'm sorry if I butted in and caused you distress. I had no right to judge your father. He is your dad in every way that counts, Zoey."

"I know. I think maybe I always wondered because of stuff my mom's folks said. But they aren't nice, so I never believed what they said about my dad." Charging ahead, Zoey said, "We saw Dad's lawyer." She looked at Mack as if asking permission to proceed, and he smiled. "The lawyer said I can choose who I want to live with. I told him I want to stay here, but I also said I really, really want you to be part of our family, J.J. I love my dad, but a dad's not a mom. When I sent the essay to your magazine any woman would do as a mom." She wrinkled her nose. "Well, not Trudy Thorne. But…you came to town and I knew I only wanted you."

"Provided you agree to marry me," Mack said. "Zoey's putting the cart before the horse." He drew J.J. tighter. "Zoey and I wrote a letter to Tom's parents and enclosed a copy of one of the photos you took. They called, but they're proceeding slowly, too. It was a shock to them, as you can imagine."

Rising on tiptoes, J.J. brushed her lips across his. "It just so happens that the check from *Her Own Woman* is just my excuse. The real reason I've come is to propose. I even brought matching wedding bands." She reached into the purse that had fallen off her shoulder and dug out a jeweler's box. Nestled inside were two gold bands, each with a trio of diamonds embedded along the top. "I guessed at your ring size, Mack."

Zoey peered in the box. "Cool rings. I can't wait for you and Dad to get married so we can be a family—a real family."

J.J. slid her gaze to Mack. "That's all I want, too," she murmured. "A wise woman named Erma Fairweather phoned to bug me. She said love trumps everything in life. I hope she's right, because I quit my job to come here."

Mack held her tenderly. "You beat me to proposing, Jill, but I want to do it properly this time, too." He sank down on one knee and took her hand. "Jilly, will you do me the honor of becoming my wife?"

Wiping away a tear she managed a husky, "I will."

Rising to face her, Mack slid his hands along her arms. Their kiss was far more than a mere brush of the lips. It was filled with love and a dollop of lust. When they broke apart they saw Zoey had dashed off and had returned with Erma, Benny and Jiggs, who barked and happily jumped around, licking J.J.'s hand.

"So…I accept your proposal, too," Mack said, lightly dusting his thumbs over her damp cheeks.

Her tears quickly turned to laughter when Zoey and the others all declared they accepted, too. "I'm home at last," she murmured.

Mack joined their hands. "You've made me the happiest man alive. I suggest we all go inside and plan a long overdue wedding."

It was Erma who said in a booming voice, "Sooner rather than later, you two. None of us are getting any younger."

* * * * *

When five o'clock hits, what happens after hours...?

0514/MB469

24 new stories from the leading lights of romantic fiction!

Featuring bestsellers Adele Parks, Katie Fforde, Carole Matthews and many more, *Truly, Madly, Deeply* **takes you on an exciting romantic adventure where love really is all you need.**

Now available at:

www.millsandboon.co.uk

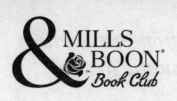 

Join the Mills & Boon Book Club

Want to read more **Cherish**™ books?
We're offering you **2 more** absolutely **FREE!**

We'll also treat you to these fabulous extras:

- 🌹 Exclusive offers and much more!

- 🌹 FREE home delivery

- 🌹 FREE books and gifts with our special rewards scheme

Get your free books now!

visit www.millsandboon.co.uk/bookclub
or call Customer Relations on 020 8288 2888

Discover more romance at

www.millsandboon.co.uk

- ❤ WIN great prizes in our exclusive competitions

- ❤ BUY new titles before they hit the shops

- ❤ BROWSE new books and REVIEW your favourites

- ❤ SAVE on new books with the Mills & Boon® Bookclub™

- ❤ DISCOVER new authors

PLUS, to chat about your favourite reads, get the latest news and find special offers:

- Find us on facebook.com/millsandboon
- Follow us on twitter.com/millsandboonuk
- ❤ Sign up to our newsletter at millsandboon.co.uk